"King's (The Blackmail Photos, 2016, etc.) four_ _ _ _ _av-elers, a husband-and-wife con art_ _ _ _ _ _ _ en artwork. . .. In this latest go-roun _ _ _ _ _ _ _ _e accustomed to author King's casua_ _ _ _ _ _ _ _ _ it comes to character development. . .. _ _ _ _ _ _ _uly written, self-contained thriller that also sets _ _age for his cons' return. Another exceptional account of heart-of-gold con artistry."—Kirkus Reviews

Treachery. Conspiracy. Murder. The Travelers, using the names Ron and Nicole Carter, break into a freeport vault to recover a stolen jewelry casket for return to a museum. Easy money. But after they're ambushed during the break-in, they must recover the casket if they're going to stay out of prison. And now a vicious gang is hot on their trail . . .

The Freeport Robbery is a noir crime thriller that will keep you on the edge of your seat. If you like nonstop action, exciting plot twists, and criminal machinations, you'll love the fourth installment of Michael P. King's Travelers series.

The Travelers

THE FREEPORT ROBBERY

THE TRAVELERS: BOOK FOUR

MICHAEL P. KING

BLURRED LINES PRESS

Blurred Lines Press

The Freeport Robbery

Michael P. King

ISBN 978-0-9861796-7-9

Cover design by Paramita Bhattacharjee at creativeparamita.com

The Freeport Robbery is a work of fiction. The names, characters, places, and events are products of the author's imagination or are used fictitiously. Any similarity to real persons or places is entirely coincidental.

For Sarah, always.

1

THE JOB

On a Friday afternoon, the Traveling Man, going by the name Ron Carter, sat in his dark blue Cadillac in the cracked asphalt parking lot of the Deal's Motel, watching the gray steel door to room 127. It was midafternoon. Sunny, with a light breeze. Not a hard day to be watching a door. But his wife, going by the name Nicole, should have come out of the room by now.

The Deal's Motel was located in the industrial part of Charles Bay, near the shipping port and the airport. Seagulls picked at trash in the nearly empty parking lot. The green neon vacancy sign in the office window flashed on and off intermittently. Up on the motel's second floor, one maid, a Latina in a black pantsuit, pushed her cleaning cart along the breezeway to the next room on her list. Ron ran his hand over his unshaven face and back through his gray-black hair. He looked at his watch. Nicole had been in the motel room with their mark for almost an hour. She should have had the credit card codes and the system passwords by now.

The mark, Pat McCall, a crooked IT manager at a credit card company—a known bad player who traded in credit card information—was, in Ron's estimation, fair game to be ripped off. Nicole had lured him out of an IT convention and brought him here without the least bit of trouble. But now the timeline was all wrong. McCall didn't look like the kind of guy who would beat a woman, but woman-beaters rarely did. Ron climbed out of the Cadillac and slipped on his gray suit coat to cover the Smith & Wesson .38 holstered on his hip. If Nicole didn't show her face in the next few minutes, he was going to knock on the door and do his detective routine.

In the room, Nicole lay naked with her shoulders back on the bed and her right leg over her left to accentuate the curve of her hips and to let McCall see her ass and her breasts at the same time. It was a porn pose that rarely failed. Her auburn hair lay loose around her shoulders. She was lean and athletic, and although she was forty-five, she appeared to be years younger. What was keeping McCall? Instead of falling asleep after he climbed off her, he'd rushed into the bath-room. So now she was on plan B: stall him until he drank the roofied water on his night table. He'd be knocked out for twelve hours. It would drastically shorten their timeline, but they would still be able to get paid for the codes and passwords before he woke up and figured out they'd been stolen. McCall came out of the bathroom wearing his black-framed glasses, his blond-gray comb-over back in place, and his huge belly hanging over his white boxer shorts.

Nicole smiled. "What's your hurry, sweetie? Come back to bed. We've got the rest of the afternoon until the mixer."

"You still here? Get out." He pointed at the motel room door.

"What?"

"If I wouldn't leave my laptop in my room at the convention center, what makes you think I'm going to give you a chance to look at it here?"

She pulled the sheet around herself as she scooted off the bed. "What brought this on? You're talking completely crazy."

"Get out."

She scooped her red lace panties and bra up off the dirty shag carpeting and crab-walked to her coffee-colored dress, which was lying over the back of the desk chair. She knew she'd lost her oppor-tunity, but she intended to leave him as confused as possible. She started to cry, sniffling at first as if she were trying to hold it back, and then moving into a full-on crying jag as she went into the bathroom to get dressed.

"You can't fool me. I know exactly what you're up to. I knew the moment you started flirting with me at the opening session."

She came out dressed, crying and blowing her nose at the same time. "You're a bastard. I hope your wife divorces you." She picked up her high heels.

"I'm already divorced."

"And now we both know why. You can't screw, and you've got a shitty personality."

She slammed the door on the way out. She walked three steps on the bare concrete of the breezeway before she bent down to pull on her high heels. "Asshole," she muttered. She took her cell phone from her handbag and dialed 911. "That little girl on the Amber Alert? I think she just went into a motel room with a man at the Deal's Motel. Fat guy with thick glasses. Room number 127."

She glanced over her shoulder just as McCall came out onto the breezeway in his boxers and grabbed her arm. "You little bitch. Where's my wallet?"

"I don't have your wallet."

Ron was about ten feet away from her, moving fast. He stepped around Nicole and gave McCall a push in the chest. McCall's comb-over fell down in his eyes. He let go of Nicole's arm. "I'm calling the cops."

Ron pointed to McCall's room and pulled the .38 from under his suit coat. McCall opened his mouth to speak. Ron cocked his head, his face neutral and his eyes empty. McCall stammered and backed into his room. Ron heard the deadbolt slide home. He turned to Nicole. "Let's get out of here."

BACK AT THEIR RENTED APARTMENT, Nicole sat on the tan rent-to-own sofa with her bare feet on the glass coffee table. Ron stood behind her, his sleeves rolled up, massaging her neck.

"It's humiliating," she said. "I thought I had him in the bag, nice little bow on top. I fucked him for nothing. Bad breath and fat-guy smell. The real problem is that he came so fast he never got winded. And now this dress stinks."

Ron held her head in both his hands and gently lifted, applying light traction before he slipped her head back and forth between his hands. "Honey, you're being too hard on yourself. This is the kind of thing that can happen when you deal with low-esteem paranoid types. Guy knew he didn't rate you. We were on a tight schedule. You didn't have time to build his ego, make him think he really had the juice."

"I'm getting too old."

He patted her shoulders, and leaned down to kiss her on the cheek. "You're not too old. You're a ball-busting siren. No one's as good at closing the deal as you. But that's beside the point. You don't have to be a player if you don't want to. We could hire a kid to do the seduction. You could do training and help me set the score."

She turned and looked up at him. "There's not going to be another woman in this crew."

"She wouldn't be competition."

"No. I won't share you with a partner. The marks—that's just work. It doesn't mean a thing. But with partners—emotions can become too powerful. And it's always two against one in a threesome."

"Do you think any woman could come between us?"

"I'm serious, Ronny. No new women. I mean it."

"Okay, I won't bring it up again. If you're uncomfortable doing the seduction, we'll just make some changes in our game."

"But no civilians."

"No civilians. Cheating civilians is always more trouble than it's worth. Especially when there are so many wannabe criminals wandering loose."

Nicole stood up. "I'm going to shower."

"That dress needs to go to the drycleaner."

"I'd rather throw it away."

"I know, but we've got to be careful with our money until we set up our next gig."

"Have you got any leads?"

"Rickover left a message on my phone. Maybe he's got something that will tide us over."

Nicole sighed. She came around the sofa, heading for the hallway to the bathroom. Ron caught her in his arms. He hugged her, rubbing her back and kissing her neck. "It's not your fault. It's all going to work out."

"I know. I'm just frustrated."

"I love you."

"I'll feel better after I shower."

He let go of her. "Think about where you want to go for supper."

SATURDAY AT 11:00 A.M., Aaron Rickover stood on the corner of Fifth and Orion in front of the Caffeination coffee shop in downtown Charles Bay, two blocks from police headquarters. The pavement was still damp from a morning rain, and the air smelled of fresh earth. He blew on his coffee between sips. Rickover was an insurance investigator for Metropolitan Assurance Company. He was forty-five, bald with a fringe of gray hair. He always wore wire-rim glasses and a winning smile. Since it was the weekend, he was dressed in new jeans, moccasins, and a blue blazer over a button-down oxford shirt. He'd been working on an investigation that he hoped would make his name and get him the promotion he needed, and now his plan was at a critical juncture.

A silver Lexus pulled up to the curb in front of him and a big redheaded man in a tight-fitting black suit stepped out of the back-seat and held the door open with his heavy, scarred hands. "Get in."

Rickover stepped toward the car. The big man shook his head. "No coffee." Rickover handed the big man his coffee before he climbed into the backseat next to the other occupant. "Mr. Philips. Good to see you."

"I wish I could say the same." Philips smiled like a hangman, his teeth gapped, and his lips rolled under. He wore a beautifully made, charcoal pinstripe suit that almost made him look trim. His wingtip shoes glowed in the gloom of the floorboard. He patted the back of the driver's seat. "Circle the block, Glen."

The Lexus pulled away from the curb, leaving the big man on the sidewalk holding the coffee cup. Rickover sat still, watching Philips, wondering just how angry he was. "Mr. Philips," he started, "no one was as surprised as me..."

Philips examined his manicure while he spoke. "No excuses. The painting you sold me was a fake. I want my money back, plus five grand for my trouble."

"Five grand?"

"You took out a loan from me and didn't even ask. Either that, or you were hoping to cheat me." He looked into Rickover's face. "Which point of view would you like me to take?"

Rickover avoided eye contact. "I don't have the money, but I'm pulling it together right now. You've got my complete attention."

"I'm not looking for effort; I'm looking for results. You may not care about your ex, but I bet you still love your kids. What would their lives be like if anything happened to you? It's a hard world to grow up in without a dad."

"Day after tomorrow I'll have your one hundred thousand."

"Really?"

"At Nohamay City."

"The tribal casino?"

"There's a freeport there. A client is going to pay me off. I'll have the cash in hand."

The Lexus pulled back to the curb. Philips nodded. "This is your only chance."

"I only need one."

The big man opened the door. Rickover started to slide out. Philips touched his arm. "Use your time wisely."

"Yes, sir."

Rickover stood on the sidewalk blinking as if he'd been in a dark basement all day. The big man chuckled, slapped him on the shoulder, pushed his coffee cup into his hand, and climbed into the Lexus, which pulled away from the curb. Rickover walked over to the brick wall by the coffee shop's picture window and stood quietly, his mind empty, trying to get his bearings. He lifted the cup to take a drink, but thought better of it, and tossed the cup into the trash can by the door. A blonde woman wearing an open tan raincoat over a short summer dress came out of the coffee shop. She looked somehow familiar, though he knew he'd never seen her before.

So far, so good. Philips wanted his money back. He'd threatened him, not his family. All he had to do was get the next part of his plan in play. He got out his phone. "Melody, how are you?"

"What's up, Aaron?"

"Can I come by and see the kids?"

"It's not your weekend. We have plans."

"Don't do this to me, Mel. I've got to go out of town. I'm not sure when I'll be back. I might have to miss next weekend."

She lowered her voice. "Always the same bullshit with you, trying to blame me for your problems. Your poor planning is not my emergency."

"I've got to work if you want the child support."

"Sure, you need to work, but your family doesn't have to come last. Your misplaced priorities are not my problem. Sober up and get your life together, or when we go to court next you'll lose your custody privileges." She hung up.

Rickover put his phone back in the pocket of his blazer. Couldn't she see that he was trying? One mistake. He got caught and now she was going to make him pay forever. Christ. Like she didn't bear some responsibility. There had to be some reason he fell into bed with Grace, something he'd been missing at home. He should have denied and lied. He might have weathered the storm. Instead, he'd let his guilt get the better of him, and now he had to pay her just to see his kids.

LATER THAT AFTERNOON, Ron and Nicole sat in Rickover's office in the

Metropolitan Assurance Building in the downtown business district. The office was ten feet by ten feet, with a window that faced another window across the street. Rickover sat in an adjustable office chair behind a standard metal office desk. His laptop was out in front of him and a stack of file folders lay on the corner of the desk. A framed certificate from the National Insurance Investigator's Association hung on the wall, and a dark-green, plastic rubber tree covered in a layer of dust pretended to grow from a wooden pot in the back right corner by the window. Ron and Nicole sat in two chrome-framed chairs facing him.

"So how you been?" Ron asked.

"I'm okay. Getting things done—know what I mean?"

"I've got to say, Aaron, that you've looked better. I'd say you're putting on weight and drinking too much."

Rickover shrugged. "Not used to living alone. But I'm working on it. I've been sleeping better. Working my list. Recommitting myself to focusing on my work."

Ron nodded. "Good for you. One day at a time."

"Yeah," Rickover said, "one day at a time." He looked at Nicole. "So how are you two doing?"

She reached over and squeezed Ron's hand. "Never better. Sometimes the bumps in the road just make your marriage stronger."

Ron gave her a quick smile before he turned back to Rickover. "So I got your message. What's the big hurry?"

"This is a really tight timeline. I need for you to do a semi-honest job."

Nicole smiled.

Rickover continued. "No, really. There's a stolen art object in a private vault out by the airport. I want you to steal it back. We return it to the museum and split the recovery fee."

Ron sat up in his chair. "Why don't you call the police?"

"The vault's in the freeport. Not enough evidence for a search warrant. Lots of VIPs store valuables there, so there's a lot of pressure for the courts not to interfere. The freeport is outside of customs, so it's technically not in the country. Anything stored there is in transit, which is why it's such a great place to store things you don't want found."

"So what's the object?"

"A gold jewel casket designed by Benvenuto Cellini. It's an important example of his early technique. It's been officially missing since World War Two, but there've always been rumors as to its whereabouts. The trail got hot recently when the current owner had to take it out of a Swiss bank after a change in international banking regulations."

"And now it's here."

Rickover nodded.

Nicole held her hands out in front of her, as if she were measuring something in space. "So this is, essentially, a Renaissance jewelry box. How big is it?"

Rickover looked down at his computer. "About ten inches by seven inches by four inches. But the foam packing and the crate make it somewhat bigger."

Nicole moved her hands around the invisible casket. "So it's for a lady's personal jewelry."

Rickover shrugged.

Nicole looked up at him. "From what I've heard, the freeport vault is like a bank vault."

"I've got the alarm codes, the access codes, and the codes for the particular locker."

"How did you come by those?" Ron asked.

"You know I can't tell you that."

"But they're good? They're the real codes?" Ron asked.

"Guaranteed."

Ron rubbed his chin. "This is a lot of moving parts. We need to spend some time studying this."

"I need you to do it ASAP."

"Meaning?"

"Tomorrow would be good."

"Sunday?"

"The vault is open business hours Monday through Friday. The casket could be on the move Monday morning. Who knows when we'll get another chance?"

"And you've got all the specs?"

"Peter Damascus Sculpture Museum in LA has the legal right to the casket. The last rightful owner willed it to the museum, even though it had been stolen. They're offering a one-hundred-fifty-thousand-dollar finder's fee. That's seventy-five thousand apiece with me handling the upfront cost."

"That's ten percent?"

"Yeah."

"So it's only worth a million and a half?"

"Who knows what it will be worth after an expert evaluation, but, yeah, that's the current figure."

"So what are the details?"

"You go in through the airport, pick up employee credentials, go into the freeport vault via the loading dock, put in the codes, meet me at the rendezvous. All the info is on this memory stick." He unplugged the memory stick from his laptop and held it up in his hand.

Ron looked at Nicole. She nodded. "Okay," he said, "you're lucky we need the cash. We're on for tomorrow. But I'm just telling you, if anything seems even the least bit wrong, we're going to bail."

"You won't regret this," Rickover said. "For you two, this is easy money."

Ron took the memory stick and put it into his jacket pocket.

"Oh," Rickover said, "almost forgot." He reached into his top desk drawer and brought out a cell phone. "Take this burner. If you need to get in touch, this is the phone to use."

Ron turned on the phone. There was one number in the contact list. He turned it off and passed it to Nicole, who put it in her handbag. "Okay," Ron said. "We'll call to set the rendezvous time. Probably be tomorrow evening."

"Super. I look forward to hearing from you."

Ron and Nicole walked down the hallway to the elevator. They waited in silence until it came. After the doors closed, Nicole said,

"Something's not right with Aaron. He was—it was almost like he was saying something he'd rehearsed."

"I know. He hasn't been himself since his wife kicked him out, but he's never led us wrong. We've always made money with him."

Neither spoke the rest of the way down. In the lobby, the lone security guard sat behind the information desk reading a newspaper. As they walked toward the glass front doors, Nicole said, "He shouldn't have hit her."

"Shouldn't have been pumping that FBI agent if he couldn't keep his mouth shut."

"He was losing it. His game had come completely off the rails. A family man has got to do better than that."

Ron held the door for her as they walked outside onto the sidewalk. The sun had come out, and the day had turned humid. The panhandler on the corner had changed shifts. "Well, she's got him by the short hairs now."

"Do you trust him?"

"Honey, the only one I trust is you."

2
_____

THE FREEPORT VAULT

S unday evening at 7:15 p.m., Ron and Nicole walked into the Charles Bay International Airport. The outer departure lobby was bustling with people standing in baggage check lines at the self-serve kiosks, blue-uniformed airline employees directing traffic, friends and relatives helping travelers get their bags from the curb to the check lines. But Ron and Nicole didn't have any bags to check. They both wore black shoes and dark blue pants that matched the security officer uniforms. Ron wore a black T-shirt and a gray pullover sweater, Nicole a black scooped-neck shirt and a jacket that matched her pants.

They walked up the escalator and got into the security line. When their turn came, they showed boarding passes for a cheap, one-hop flight to Philadelphia and produced IDs that showed them to be James and Lydia Morrison. The TSA agent marked their boarding passes with a yellow marker and waved them through. They emptied their pockets into plastic containers and placed the containers on the conveyer and took their turns in the scanner, holding up their arms while the machine worked around them. Then they put on their shoes and turned left down the hallway to the C gates. At the second door, marked Restricted Access, Ron punched in the access code and opened the door, which led into an industrial hallway. At the end of the hallway, they turned into a room on the right, which was lined with rows of lockers. Ron opened locker number 259. Inside were two airport security officer shirts, IDs, and holstered pistols. They put their security officer shirts on over their shirts, attached their IDs to their pockets, and put their jackets into the locker.

Nicole looked Ron over critically. "Button your top shirt button."

"Thanks."

"What about me?"

"You look great."

She ejected the clip on her nine-millimeter pistol, checked the breech to make sure there wasn't a round in the chamber, and pushed the clip back in. "So far, so good."

"Rickover has never let us down. There's plenty of stuff to be paranoid about without being paranoid about him."

"A wise man once told me better safe than sorry."

"And I intend to take my advice."

They went out the other side of the locker-room and down a set of metal steps onto the tarmac, which was loud with the rumble of jet engines, the sound of baggage carts, and the steady beep of safety alarms. Night was coming on, but the airfield was brightly lit. To their right they could see a number of planes sitting at gates. To their left they could see an open area framed by a chain-link fence with barbed wire along the top. Just then, a small yellow utility truck pulled up, and a young, dark-skinned maintenance worker with ear protection hanging around his neck climbed out. "Hey," he said, "I don't know you. Where's Blount?"

Ron stuck out his hand. "I don't know you, either. I'm Bill. I don't know Blount. I just go where they send me."

The man shook hands with him. "I hear you. I'm Terry." He looked at Nicole.

"I'm Erica." They shook hands.

"I guess you two don't usually work Sundays?"

"No, first time for both of us."

"It'll get quiet around ten."

"Good to know."

"Well, I'm off. You two working tomorrow?"

"Definitely."

"See you later."

The man went up the steel steps. Ron and Nicole waited until they heard the door bang shut; then they put on their latex gloves and hurried to the utility truck. The keys were in it. Nicole followed the yellow lane on the tarmac to get to the gate in the chain-link fence. The tarmac grew quieter and darker as they drove away from the terminal. The gate, which was wide enough for a semitruck, was set on rollers. A light and a surveillance camera were up on a pole to the right of the lock. Ron put on his black ski mask before he jumped out, put in the code on the lock, and rolled the gate open. Nicole drove through. He closed the gate and got back in the truck.

"Which way?" Nicole asked.

Ron looked at a map on his smartphone. He pointed to their left, toward a group of industrial buildings. "That's a warehouse. The next one as well. The brick one is ours."

She drove over to the line of buildings. As they neared, they could read the signs: Clemens Storage, Elephant Transportation Solutions, Premium Security Transit.

"That's it."

The front of Premium Security Transit looked like a bank. Brick and limestone, large plate-glass windows, a row of car parking. They drove down the driveway between Elephant Transportation Solutions and Premium Security Transit, and turned into the alley behind the buildings. The back of Premium Security was a stark concrete wall with a loading dock and a gray steel access door. Spotlights and two cameras guarded the entry points. A yellow forklift sat on the loading dock. Nicole parked the utility truck facing out. She put on her ski mask before she followed Ron up the steps to the door. "The moment of truth," he whispered.

He input the door code, moved into a dimly lit bay half full of large cardboard boxes stacked on pallets, and input the alarm codes on the panel just inside the door. The computer turned off the sound and motion sensors, as well as the interior cameras, and turned on the emergency lighting.

"We're in business."

He looked at the building map on his smartphone. They went through a door into a short hall with offices on each side, and then through another door to the front of the building, where employees dealt with clients. The walls were marble, the desks were polished hard wood, and the chairs looked plush. Through the front windows they could see the client parking and, in the distance, the main gates to this area from the street outside the airport. They moved across this room to a shiny chrome security door. Ron input the code. They went into a large room lined with lockers, some the size of PO boxes, some the size of closets or storage rooms. The floor and ceiling were smooth concrete. Down the center of the room was a row of bar-height tables, some with stools. Ron took a pencil flashlight from his pocket and began reading off the numbers on the lockers. They found the one they were looking for about two-thirds the way back, in a group of closet-size lockers. He input the door code. On the floor of the closet was a wooden packing crate about one and a half feet by one foot by two-thirds of a foot. Ron squatted to get his arms around it. "Jesus, this is heavier than I expected. Casket itself must be twenty pounds, easy."

"I can see you're starting to think crazy." Nicole stepped out of the doorway so that he could carry the packing crate to the nearest table.

"I know, I know. The kicker is that we can't melt it down and sell it. Too much value is tied up in what it is. But just thinking about it gets my blood pumping."

She shut the door to the locker.

He pulled a small prying bar out of his back pocket, levered the top off the crate, and lifted away a piece of two-inch, white foam. "Sweet baby Jesus."

Nicole put her hand on his shoulder as she stepped forward to look. The top of the casket glowed the color of honey. Intricate flowers were engraved over its surface, the centers of which looked as if they had once contained jewels of some sort. She shook her head as if coming out of a trance and glanced at her watch. "We're running late."

"Got you." Ron gently laid the foam back onto the casket and tapped the top of the crate back on with his fist. Nicole shook out a black duffel bag. They slipped the bag around the crate, and carried it out the way they came, each holding one handle, taking care to close the doors they had opened along the way.

At the back door, Nicole stood with the bag on the loading dock and scanned the alley for trouble while Ron reset the alarm system. The forklift sat on the loading dock, the utility truck sat in the parking, two green dumpsters sat by the back doors of the building across the alley, and a pallet of concrete blocks sat to the right of the loading dock. Ron pushed the door shut and gave her a confident nod. They picked up the duffel.

As they started down the steps, a man stepped out from behind the left dumpster wearing a Kevlar vest and holding an AR15 assault rifle. His red beard stuck out from the bottom of his black ski mask. "That's far enough," he said.

Ron and Nicole reached for their automatic pistols. Four more men appeared in the alley, two to the left and two to the right, all masked and armed like the first man. The bearded man continued. "You don't have to die here. Give us the bag, and we'll be on our way."

Ron and Nicole shared a glance. They were still holding the bag between them and still holding their pistols.

"I know what you're thinking. It's not worth it. You won't get out of here."

"You can't risk damaging the box," Ron said.

"Look, no hard feelings. This is just work. Do the math. The only way you leave here is if you give up that duffel bag."

"What's to stop you from killing us after we give you the box?"

"We don't need to, for starters. We don't need the noise, and dumping two bodies is a lot of work. We can't kill you and just leave you here."

Ron and Nicole walked down the remaining steps to the alley and set the duffel bag on the pavement. The man nodded. "Now you're making sense. Set your guns on the ground."

Ron and Nicole crouched down, but instead of setting down their guns, they dove for the utility truck and scrambled up behind it as the hijackers opened fire and retreated to the cover of the dumpsters and the pallet of concrete blocks. "We're outgunned," Ron said. "But there was no way I was going to put my life in their hands."

"I figured as much."

Ron yelled to the bearded man, "Now you can take the duffel."

The men behind the pallet of concrete blocks kept firing, pinning Ron and Nicole behind the truck, while one of the men from the right dumpster ran over to the duffel and grabbed it up by both handles. As he started to hump it away, Ron got off a lucky shot and caught him in the leg. He stumbled to the pavement. Then the two men behind the concrete blocks stepped out, continuously firing as they moved across Nicole's line of fire to get to the front of the truck.

The bearded man yelled, "Grab him and the duffel and let's get out of here."

The men at the front of the truck poured fire down both sides, while their partners collected their man and the duffel bag. Ron and Nicole were hunkered down behind the truck tires at the back of the truck, unable to return fire, bullets swarming past them and ricocheting off the concrete wall behind them like angry wasps. They were making themselves small, watching under the truck bed for approaching legs, waiting for the moment the two hijackers would appear on both sides of them with their assault rifles blazing. Suddenly, the firing stopped. Their ears were ringing. Ron peeked around the side of the truck. The hijackers were gone. Ron tapped Nicole's shoulder and pointed. They came out of the loading zone just as the last hijacker disappeared around the corner. "Let's use the truck," Ron said.

"Are we really going to do this?"

"You hurt?"

"Just a few nicks."

"Luck is on our side."

They got in the utility truck, Ron driving, rolled slowly up to the intersection of two alleys, and turned. The hijackers were jogging toward a white Ford Transit, the front two carrying the duffel, the red-bearded man with his arm around the wounded man, and the fifth man covering their retreat. Ron stopped the truck and threw open the door. The fifth man opened fire. Ron crouched behind the door and returned fire. The men carrying the duffel looked over their shoulders.

"Keep moving," the bearded man said.

He helped the wounded man to the pavement and started back down the alley, zigzagging from wall to wall, firing as he came. The fifth man was on one knee in the middle of the alley, his rifle at his shoulder. Their combined fire was pounding the front of the truck into scrap metal. Nicole lay on the floorboard. Her door was stuck. The windshield shattered, raining tiny chunks of safety glass down on her. Ron dove onto the floorboard, grabbed her by the arm, and pulled her into the driver's side. "We're getting murdered here. Put it in reverse and press on the gas."

She reached up, shoved the shifter into reverse, and pressed on the gas with both hands. The truck started rolling backward on two flat tires, whap, whap, whap, no one holding the wheel. Ron hung from the door and kept firing on the kneeling man, who finally fell sideways. The front of the truck listed to the right until the left back bumper hit the alley wall. Ron dropped to the pavement and rolled under the truck door. As he came to his feet, the bearded hijacker punched him in the head, knocking him into the wall. He slid down to the pavement. The hijacker snapped open a lock-back knife with a flick of his wrist. Ron saw an eagle tattoo on the back of the man's hand. The knife blade swooped down in a backhand motion, heading for Ron's throat. Ron threw up his arms.

Nicole fell out of the truck and scampered under the door. Just a few feet away, she saw the bearded man standing over Ron. She sprang up and charged, catching the hijacker off-balance in midswing. They fell in a tangle; the knife flew free. She landed on top, scrambled off him, and pulled her pistol as she stepped back.

The hijacker was on his feet, starting toward her. She fired twice, somehow missing him. He pushed past her and ran back to where the fifth man lay. He grabbed him by his vest and dragged him down the alley. The other two hijackers were already carrying the man with the leg wound. They all hurried toward the Ford Transit.

Nicole looked down at Ron. "Are you okay?"

"Just have to catch my breath."

Police sirens howled in the distance. Nicole held out her hand. "We have to go."

Ron grabbed her hand, put his other hand on the wall, and got to his feet. She gripped his shoulders and looked him in the eye. "Are you sure you're okay?"

"Just feeling old. But look at you, wearing your superhero suit and everything."

"This is no time to kid. I was afraid you were stabbed."

"I'm okay, Nicki. You can let go."

"I can't believe I missed that guy point-blank."

"It happens. Lucky he ran out of ammo." He watched the Transit disappear around a corner. "There goes the casket." He turned and looked at the bullet-ridden truck. "And we won't be following. Let's check for evidence and make our way to the rendezvous."

"Think it's safe?"

"It's the only way I know to get out of here."

The inside of the truck was broken glass, torn upholstery, and shell casings—nothing that could lead back to them. They jogged back to the loading dock, hyperaware, guns out, expecting an ambush behind every dumpster or blind spot, but they were alone. The loading dock behind the vault was just more pocked concrete, smashed hollow-point bullets, and shell casings. The police sirens were getting louder.

They took a left down another alley between two warehouses, took off their security guard shirts and put them in a dumpster that reeked of used machine oil, and started jogging. Every few blocks, Ron checked their location on his smartphone until they came out behind an old, brick warehouse with flaking white paint. Across a hundred yards of weeds, old tractor-trailer tires, twisted steel cable, and rusty sheet metal parts was the chain-link fence to the private airfield. A long row of airplane hangars backed up to the fence. At the third fence post they checked, the chain-link had been cut just high enough for them to crawl through. Once inside the airfield, they stayed in the shadows as they moved between the hangars, until they came to the one with "Learn to fly with Bob" painted in red on the side. The side door under the green awning was locked. The customer parking was empty.

"Looks like Aaron is an asshole," Nicole said.

"Let me try the burner," Ron said. He took out the throwaway cell phone that Rickover had given them and called the only number in the address book. It rolled over to a message that the voice mail hadn't been set up. He put the phone back in his pocket. "Nothing." He took out his own phone and speed-dialed Rickover's cell phone. The voice mail asked him to leave a message. "And his regular phone is off."

He glanced up and down the street. "We better ditch these guns and get indoors."

They wiped off the guns and holsters and put them in the trash barrel by the customer parking, and then took off their latex gloves and put them in their pockets. They walked along the backs of the airplane hangars, staying out of the view of surveillance cameras, until they could see the front gate of the airfield. Ron called a taxi. They stood in the shadow and waited. Nicole dusted off her pants. "So you think Aaron set us up?"

"It's either that, or someone else was trying for the same object at the same time on the same day."

"You think it's that bad? Really? After all the work we've done with him?"

"Maybe he's dead. Maybe it went sideways from what he planned, and he couldn't get in touch. Right now we have no way of knowing what's what; all I know is we need to get paid."

A yellow taxi pulled up to the gate of the airfield. Ron and Nicole walked out the gate and got into the cab. The cabbie, an elderly black man wearing a gray cap, didn't even bother to look over his shoulder. "Where to?"

They gave an address a few blocks from their apartment. The cabbie pulled away from the curb. "Waiting long?"

"No," Nicole said.

"Had a hard time getting in here. Hell of a jam at the main airport. Cops all over the place. Traffic will be backed up for an hour at least. Lucky there's the cutoff from this side."

"Lucky we didn't fly commercial," Nicole replied.

AFTER THE CABBIE dropped them off, they stood on the sidewalk and watched him drive away before they walked up one block and over two more to their apartment building. There was no one suspicious on the street. All the streetlamps were working just fine. The living room light in their second-floor apartment was on, just as they had left it, and there were no strange shadows in the room. The downstairs door was locked, just as it should be, and the stairwell was quiet. Their neighbors were all civilians with regular jobs, so they were all tucked in for the night. Ron and Nicole stopped outside their door and listened. Nothing. The toothpick that Ron had broken off in the crack between the door and the doorjamb was still there.

"We're good."

He pushed open the door and let Nicole in first. She pulled her black top off over her head and kicked her shoes and her pants off onto the oak floor on her way to the bathroom. Ron bolted the door. He emptied his pockets into the blue bowl on the side table under the light switch. Then he pulled off his T-shirt and pants, dropped them on the floor next to Nicole's clothes, and padded into the kitchenette to get a garbage bag from the under sink cabinet. He shoved their clothes into the bag and then carried it into the bathroom to retrieve her underwear and socks. He could see her in the shower through the glass door. He took off his own underwear and socks and put them in the bag before he tossed the bag out of the bathroom and shut the door. "Hey."

From inside the shower, she replied, "Hey."

He opened the shower door and stepped in. She moved over. Her head was under the spray. Soapy water ran down her body and swirled in the drain at her feet. "Let me look at you."

She moved out from under the spray and turned slowly with her eyes closed. He took her hand. "Scraped elbow. Pretty big bruise on your hip. A number of little nicks." He raised her hand to his lips and kissed it.

She opened her eyes. "Your turn."

He turned in a slow circle. She put her hand on his chest and maneuvered him under the spray. "Bruise on your shoulder blade. Flesh wound on your left side. From the look of your right knee, you might be limping tomorrow. Lots of little cuts, but no purple heart for you, mister."

She got the soap off the shelf and started washing his back while he shampooed his hair. When he'd finished rinsing his head, she said, "I'm pretty angry."

He turned to face her. "What about?"

She handed him the soap. He started washing the rest of his body. "You almost died today."

"Don't exaggerate. It was a close thing, but it didn't happen." He put the soap back on the shelf and rinsed off.

"That was more than just a close thing."

He pulled her into the spray. "You're right. You angry with me for being a testosterone-fueled idiot? For not just walking away?"

She shook her head. "I ought to be, but I'm not. They might have killed us if we'd laid down our guns."

He ran his hand up and down her arm. "So, what?"

"I'm angry with Aaron. I want to see him hurt. I want him to feel what I felt right then, when I thought I was too late."

"Me too." He kissed her lips and held her tight, the spray falling down on them.

Then she said, "That's what I feel, and it's been a long time since I've felt so crazy angry to kill someone. I got to say it scares me."

He took her face in his hands. "I'm going to take care of you," he said. "We're in a bad patch. But our relationship and our professionalism will carry us through. It always has. Us, together—we always save each other."

They kissed. She pushed him against the tile wall and reached down between his legs. He turned off the water. "Bad knee, remember?"

She opened the shower door and pulled him out onto the rug in front of the shower stall. They kissed again, their hands moving with the comfortable knowledge of each other's body, falling into rhythm as they rolled back and forth across the rug. Afterward, they toweled each other off. "You hungry?" he said. "I'm hungry. We've got to go out. Let's get something to eat."

Nicole hung up her towel. "Who's still open?"

"Nina's is open twenty-four seven."

She squeezed his hand. "Pancakes and eggs?"

"You got it."

She kissed him lightly. "What about Aaron?"

"We'll deal with him tomorrow."

They parked the Cadillac in the on-street parking at Cabot Park, a small city park across the street from Nina's, an all-night diner where they liked the coffee. Ron got out of the passenger's side with the trash bag containing their clothes from the job tucked under his arm. Nicole waited at the curb while he dumped the bag in a park trash can. Then they crossed the street holding hands.

Nina's was a traditional diner, with a long counter and bar stools running the length of the back and a row of red vinyl booths along the front windows. The place was empty. They slid into one of the booths where they had a good view of the park. The waitress, a middle-aged woman wearing a sunflower yellow uniform that smelled of cigarette smoke, brought an insulated pitcher of coffee and glasses of water when she came to take their order. "Glad to see you folks," she said.

"Glad you're open," Ron replied.

She pulled her pad from her apron. "What'll it be?"

Ron looked at Nicole. She nodded. "Pancakes and eggs over easy, patty sausage, glass of milk."

"Me, too," he said.

In a few minutes, their food arrived. Ron slid his sausage off its plate and onto the plate with his pancakes and eggs. He scooped the whipped butter out of the paper container and smeared it across the top of his pancakes. Then he poured syrup over everything, including his eggs. Nicole shook her head. "I never get used to watching you eat breakfast."

"This isn't a five-star restaurant, okay?"

"Whatever." She cut her eggs into bite-size pieces and ate them first. They sat there, eating slowly, enjoying the pleasure of eating, not saying anything to each other, just watching the park without seeming to watch the park. When Nicole stopped eating, half her sausage and most of her pancakes were still on the plates. Ron's plate only had a few bites of pancake left. "I'm done," she said. "Do you want any of mine?"

"I'm full," he said, but he speared the sausage onto his plate. Just then, over in the park, they saw a gray-bearded man, wearing a coat and pushing a shopping cart, stop at the park trash can, pull out their bag of clothes, and put it in his cart. Ron tapped his fingers on the table. "Mission accomplished. Let's just pay at the counter."

AT AN INTERSTATE REST stop north of the city, the white Ford Transit sat in a parking space far away from the building and the other cars that were coming and going in the dark. A "dog-walking area" sign was posted in the nearby grass and three empty concrete picnic tables were close at hand. The sprinkler system was watering the grass, the hissing of the water competing with the chirping of the insects. The red-bearded man, dressed in old jeans, a black T-shirt and work boots, his long hair pulled back in a ponytail, leaned against the side of the van smoking a cigarette.

A Camry pulled into the space one car over, and Aaron Rickover got out. "Tommy," he said.

Tommy threw down his cigarette. "What the fuck, Aaron? That was some bullshit you sent us on."

Rickover held his hands up and took a step back. "Hey, calm down. What happened?"

"That guy who was supposed to fold up? He went Rambo on us. Lost two of my guys."

"Did you put him down?"

Tommy shook his head.

"Christ, Tommy, it was five to two. And an ambush."

"You didn't tell us his partner was a woman."

"What difference does that make?" Rickover patted his hands together and sucked on his lip. "How noisy was it?"

"It was noisy. We barely got out of there ahead of the cops."

"This job was supposed to be completely under the radar. No police involvement."

"Fuck you."

"But you got the box?"

"Yeah, we got it."

Rickover reached into the inside pocket of his blue blazer and pulled out an envelope. "Here's your down payment."

Tommy glared at him.

"Hey," he said, "I'm sorry about your guys. I gave you the best info I had." He waved the envelope in his hand.

"You're an asshole," Tommy said.

"Yeah, probably. But we're here to make money, right? And you won't make any if you don't give me the box."

Tommy opened the side door on the Transit, unzipped the duffel, and held it open so that Rickover could see the wooden crate.

"Excellent. Bring it over." Rickover opened the Camry's trunk. Tommy hugged the duffel over to the Camry. Rickover handed him the envelope. "Just like always. You'll get the rest of your cut as soon as it's sold. A week or two, max."

"It's still a load of bullshit."

"I wish it went differently, but there's nothing I can do about it now." He stuck out his hand. "No hard feelings."

Tommy knocked his hand away. "You didn't lose two friends today."

"I'll be in touch." Rickover got back into his car.

LYING in the weeds up on the hill in the dark, Grace Mosley, an FBI agent specializing in stolen art, took one last picture of the red-bearded man and Rickover. Then she put the lens cap back on her camera and waited for the Camry and the Transit to leave the rest stop. After she saw the Transit's taillights disappear onto the interstate, she stood up, rolled up the blanket she'd been lying on, and made her way carefully through the brush and dry weeds back down to the parking lot, where her car was waiting.

Thirty minutes later, she was at her condo, a two-bedroom in a recently built gated community on the north side of the city, standing at the black granite counter that divided her kitchen from her living room area, swirling a glass of red wine. Grace was forty-three years old. She looked good and she knew it. She wasn't thin anymore, but she carried the hard muscle of a middle-aged athlete. She was still dressed for work. Her dark hair was tied back at her neck; she wore a black pants suit with a white, open-collared shirt. A small gold cross hung from a thin chain around her neck. Rickover sat on the sofa facing her, his blue blazer lying on the arm of a nearby easy chair, a glass of wine in front of him on the coffee table. "Okay," she started, "I've been patient. I took the pictures for you. What's this all about?"

Rickover took a minute to wipe his glasses with his handkerchief. "You know how I've been investigating the use of freeports to stash stolen art. I've developed a cover as a crook to gather evidence."

"Risky move."

"You know how my situation is. With the divorce, I need a raise. I'm topped out. To get a raise, I've got to get a promotion." He sipped his wine. "Anyway, Philips figured out that the painting I sold him was a forgery. He wants his money back, which forced my hand. So I faked the theft of the Cellini casket to put my plan in motion."

"That was your shit show out at the airport?"

"Yeah. Turned out to be a little messy, but my guys got the casket. Out at the rest stop? You took pictures of the handover."

"Local cops know what you're up to?"

"Can't trust them."

"You shouldn't mess with Philips; you know that, don't you? If he finds out about you, you're dead. You should just pay him and buy the time to work your other leads."

"Look, Philips is on me, and I don't have the money to pay him. Besides, all I have to do is take the casket to the rendezvous with the buyer at the Nohamay freeport vault and then wait for Philips to come for his money."

"Why there? Isn't that tribal land?"

"The Nohamay Nation has a casino and a freeport down in the corner of their reservation. It's all run by a Singaporean corporation. NewTrust. No cops at all—just security personnel, which is why Philips feels safe keeping a locker in the vault there. Only the FBI has jurisdiction, and the corporation is prickly about anyone stepping on its turf, so they fight every search warrant. But when you arrest Philips in Nohamay City for trafficking in stolen art—"

"When *I* arrest him?"

"Consider it a present. Anyway, then we'll have probable cause to search his vault locker. And once we get into his locker, we'll have all the evidence we need to put him away for good. We'll get Philips and the buyer, and we'll get the casket back."

"I wish you'd reconsider." She sat down next to him. "Sure, if this works, you'll be the stuff of legends. No doubt. But if you lose the casket, you'll go to jail. And if Philips finds out, he'll kill you. There's got to be another way."

He shook his head. "It's going to work. I need a big win to solve my problems. I've been playing it safe way too long."

Mosley set her wine on the coffee table. "When was the last time you saw your kids?"

"Three weeks ago. I missed last week and Melody won't let me switch weekends."

"How are they doing?"

"Okay, I guess. The girls didn't see me that much before, so I don't know if it's that big a deal."

"That's stupid talk. Of course they miss you. You've got to find the time to be their dad."

He drank some wine. "As soon as I'm done with this case, I'll make supervisor. Then I'll be able to make some changes." He set his glass down. "What about you? How's your daughter doing?"

Mosley smiled. "Kelly's talking in sentences now."

"Really?"

"Yeah. The teachers at Clear Skies are amazing. It's been less than a year, and you wouldn't believe the change. At her old school—don't get me started. Every year she fell farther behind."

"Must cost a fortune."

"One-on-one tutoring isn't cheap. Even with the scholarship, money is tight."

"Is Kelly's father helping?"

"That rat bastard? He fell out of the picture a long time ago. You don't want to be that asshole, Aaron. You've got to make time for your kids."

He nodded. Then he reached over and fingered the gold cross hanging at her throat. She leaned forward to kiss him, but he let go of the necklace and shifted his head. "I thought you were going to spend the night," she said.

"I have to catch the red-eye."

"It's not because your wife found out about us?"

"Is that what you think?" He took her chin in his hand and gave her a quick kiss before he stood up. "I don't blame you. I'm the one who cheated on my wife. My timeline is just too tight tonight."

"The one thing I feel bad about is you losing your kids."

"Don't. Everything will be fixed up before you know it. Ten days, max. When you swoop in for the arrest, it'll more than make things right." He looked at his watch. "I've got to go."

Mosley walked him to the door. They kissed again. "Be careful," she said, "and if things go sideways, don't try to fix it yourself. Call me right away."

. . .

BACK AT THEIR APARTMENT, Ron turned on the late news on the TV in their bedroom while hanging up his clothes. "Breaking news. Robbery at Premium Security Transit," the newscaster said.

Ron stepped out of the closet in his underwear and his unbuttoned shirt, picked up the remote, and turned up the volume. "Nicki."

Nicole came into the bedroom wearing a T-shirt and boxer shorts, her toothbrush in her mouth. The newscaster continued, "Police and FBI responded to gunfire at the Charles Bay Freeport this evening, where at least one item, a rare art object in transit to the Peter Damascus Sculpture Museum in Los Angeles, was stolen. There will be more information after an inventory of Premium Security Transit is completed."

Ron turned off the TV and threw the remote down on the bed. "Fuck, fuck, fuck."

Nicole went into the bathroom, rinsed her mouth, and came back. "So Aaron really did screw us."

Ron picked up his smartphone and redialed Rickover. The call rolled over to voice mail. "Still no answer. I'm going to kill him in so many ways," Ron said. "Stealing back something that was stolen is one thing, but we would never take a straight-up job stealing art, and Aaron knows it. You can't sell the stuff. There's too much notoriety. With the media coverage, the Feds are going to be all over this. This is exactly why we don't steal from civilians. And then sending that crew to rob us so he wouldn't have to pay us."

"Let's get out of town. Deal with Aaron later."

"And run where? We're bound to be on surveillance footage somewhere. Did you always have your mask down? What about driving across the tarmac? What about after we ditched the shirts? And let's not forget about the mechanic we met at the gate area. The FBI is going to put everything under a microscope. As soon as they get our pictures, they'll be plastered all over the country. We won't be able to work anywhere. Our only chance is to get the casket back before the Feds settle on us. Once the casket is returned, there'll be no incentive for them to keep working the case, and they'll need to move on to something hot."

"Okay," Nicole said, "so we pack a bag tonight in case the whole thing blows up, and we find Aaron and squeeze him."

MOSLEY LOCKED her front door and wandered back into the living room, trying to decide what she should do about Aaron. She looked at his wine glass sitting next to hers on the coffee table, and she saw him sitting there on her sofa. He talked a good game, but he was grasping at straws. The idea that he would make supervisor even if he arrested Philips was ludicrous. She couldn't think of a single super- visor at Metropolitan Assurance Company who didn't have a management degree of some kind. And he didn't have the slightest idea of what was really going on. He'd have a coronary if he found out that Philips was the source of the money she used to pay her daughter's tuition at Clear Skies. She picked up his wine glass and drank off the last of his wine. Maybe she'd be able to help Aaron from the periphery, keep him from getting himself killed or arrested or fired. They were friends, after all. And his kids and his ex were counting on him. She set his glass down. That's what she would do. Her daughter had to come first, but she'd help him as best she could.

She got out her extra phone. "Mr. Philips? It's me. Rickover is setting a trap for you."

"Don't worry. I'm on it. I'm trying to keep you in the clear."

"He's dealt me in—wants me to make the arrests."

"Is that right?" The line was quiet.

"Mr. Philips?"

"I'm here. Give me a second." The line was quiet for a few more minutes. "This is what I want you to do. Go to Nohamay City. Do your normal thing. Check in with Clare."

"He's got the casket, so we can probably get your money."

"Let me worry about my business. Some of my guys are going to clean up this mess. You just go there and be ready. When we need you, we'll be in touch."

The line went dead. She looked at the screen on her phone. How did everything get so complicated? She felt guilty about Aaron. She'd made friends with him because Philips had asked her to find out what he knew, but she'd started sleeping with him by accident. On the day she took Kelly to live at Clear Skies, Kelly had started wailing and banging her head against the wall in the lobby when she left her with her new resident counselor. Her old school, where they didn't have enough staff to help her, was the only home Kelly had ever known. She loved her caregivers. So even though Mosley knew she was doing the right thing, she felt like a traitor to her daughter. Driving back into town, she couldn't face being alone in her condo.

She called Aaron, who met her at Davy's Bar and Grill to talk shop, and they started pounding down drinks. She didn't remember coming home that night. She woke up at dawn snuggled up against Aaron on the living room carpet with her blouse unbuttoned and her underwear missing. Of course, she hadn't forced him to cheat on his wife. But she should have cut off the sex before it became a crutch in their relationship and Melody became suspicious. That had been a mistake. He'd screwed up his marriage, and now she was his closest friend. Poor bastard didn't stand a chance. If only her insurance provided coverage for private residential programs. Or she really did have a scholarship. Still, she had to stick with the choice she had made. Kelly was doing so much better. She couldn't send her back to that overcrowded public facility.

Ron and Nicole parked on the street in front of Rickover's apartment building, a five-story in a run-down apartment complex. Rickover lived in a studio apartment on the first floor. Kids' bikes were chained to the rusty wrought-iron fence that ran along the sidewalks, and trash bags were piled up on top of the steel trash cans that were set out at the curb. One of the outside lights was broken, and the building door was slightly ajar. Ron went in ahead of Nicole, his hand around the .38 he carried in the flap pocket of his sports coat. The hall was deserted. The carpet was worn and stained, but the hall smelled of fresh paint. "So, what's it going to be?" Ron whispered. "Good cop, bad cop? Gun to the head? Empty his pockets?"

Nicole shrugged. "We'll just have to see where he's at. If he'll play straight, we can play straight."

"I think you're a little optimistic, but I'll follow your lead."

They counted off the apartment numbers until they came to Rickover's apartment. Ron pressed the doorbell, waited, then pressed again. No footsteps. He knocked. Waited. No footsteps. Nicole looked down the hall. "All clear."

Ron picked the deadbolt. It was surprisingly simple, considering Rickover's profession. He opened the door slowly. "Aaron," he said.

He stuck his head in and turned on the light. The place was a pigsty. The bed was unmade. Dirty clothes littered the floor. Old newspapers, pizza boxes, and soft drink and beer cans were strewn across the sofa and coffee table. The kitchenette counter was completely covered in dirty dishes. Nicole looked in the closet. Shoes on the floor, clothes hanging on hangers. Ron looked in the bathroom. Clutter on the counters. Dry bath towel on the rack. He came back into the living area. "Nothing here."

"It would take an anthropologist to figure out what normal was in this mess." Nicole picked up a cereal bowl off the counter and set it back down.

"So all we know is we can't find Aaron. Either he's selling the casket, or that rip-off crew dumped him in a hole somewhere before they came for us."

Nicole opened the refrigerator. "Milk is still good for another week."

"Meaning what? The only other lead we have is eagle tattoo guy. We've got to find him. And we won't be able to do that tonight." Ron frowned. "The next two days are crucial. I wish we had more to go on, but this is all we've got."

They walked back out onto the sidewalk. The street was quiet. "Going to be hard to find eagle tattoo guy," Nicole said. "All we know is he has red hair, a beard long enough to stick out of his mask, and an eagle tattoo on the back of his hand."

Ron used the fob to open the car. "We know he's a big guy in good shape, military-trained, who's an armed robber who hangs out with a crew of armed robbers."

Nicole glanced over her shoulder as she opened the car door. "Check out sporting goods guy in your rearview mirror."

Ron adjusted his mirror to look. A good-looking black guy with a conservative haircut, dressed in chinos and a red golf shirt, was standing at the bus stop. "Okay."

"Doesn't quite fit in around here, does he? Now look at his brother sitting on the stoop, one, two, three houses up the street, yellow siding with white trim. Big guy, black-framed glasses, khakis, and a green and blue-striped shirt."

Ron readjusted his mirror for driving and glanced toward the house that Nicole had indicated. "If I see one more, I'm going to think I'm in a sci-fi movie. We must not be the only ones checking up on Aaron. Let's get out of here before they take notice of us."

3

ON THE RUN

Nicole came into the living room dressed for the day while Ron was loading his breakfast dishes into the dishwasher. Outside, the occasional beeping of a garbage truck backing into an alley interrupted the low hum of neighborhood traffic. "Good morning, sweetie."

She sat on a stool at the counter. Ron shut the dishwasher, poured coffee into two cups, and set one cup in front of her. "How was your sleep?" he asked.

"Slept great. Not even stiff this morning."

"I'm still creaking a little bit, but I'm getting there."

"Any new thoughts on today's program?"

He shook his head. "We've got to just start at the beginning. Make this as simple as possible. Find the casket. Change our luck."

She sipped her coffee. "Got your phone?"

He dug his smartphone out of his pants pocket and passed it to her. She called Rickover's phone. No answer; no voice mail. She called Rickover's office.

"Metropolitan Assurance Company."

"Aaron Rickover, please."

"One moment."

The phone rang. No one answered. She let it ring. Finally the call transferred to voice mail. She hung up. "He's not answering his phone, and he's not at work."

"Let's take one more look at his apartment."

The on-street parking was still full on both sides of the street in front of their apartment. Across the street, two moms—one white and one black—sat on a porch drinking coffee while their toddlers rode identical tricycles up and down the sidewalk. A contractor's truck was already in the driveway of the white house halfway up the block. Builder making an early start. Then Nicole noticed a hard-muscled blond man, dressed in chinos and a blue golf shirt, standing at the corner as if he were waiting for a taxi. "Don't look, but there's another sporting goods guy."

"You know him?" Ron asked.

"Never seen him before."

They got into their car and circled around the block. There was another white man—brown hair, beer belly, and a red and blue rugby shirt—walking down the alley behind their apartment building.

Ron shook his head. "There's no way we were followed back from Aaron's."

"Let's get out of here. See if they follow us."

Ron drove into the downtown business district. The traffic was stop and go. Crowds of pedestrians crossed at the corners when the lights changed. Nicole looked up from the map on her phone. "Take a right into the alley halfway up the next block."

The light changed. Ron drove up into the next block, saw the alley, and turned. It was one-way, with dumpsters and cars parked along the edges on both sides, but there was enough room for them to squeeze through. Nicole was watching out the back window. Ron pulled up to the next street. "Take a left," she said.

"Going to be a bitch," he replied. A produce truck rolled by. He saw a gap between a minivan and a red Camry, stepped on the gas, shot across the oncoming lane, and hit the brakes while the Caddie was at an angle in the stopped traffic in the right lane.

"Good job," Nicole said. "Didn't see anyone, but if they were behind us, they're screwed now."

They drove north until the businesses began to have their own parking lots, pulled into a Caffeination coffee shop, and parked facing the street. "Okay," Ron said, "let's think this through. Were those guys really watching our apartment?"

"The black guys at Aaron's were definitely on stake-out."

"Yeah."

Nicole continued. "If I hadn't seen them, I wouldn't have noticed the white guys. Might have thought they were apartment-hunting or something."

"Maybe they were."

"The way our luck has been running? You've got to be kidding."

"If they were set up on our apartment, how did they find us? They didn't follow us from Aaron's, and they weren't cops."

"Nobody was following us from the airport, right?"

Ron nodded. "There's no way anyone could find the taxi. And the homeless guy got the clothes. If those guys belonged to Aaron, we would have been ambushed as soon as we got home."

"Aaron..." Nicole's eyes lit up. "The phone. Where's the burner Aaron gave us? The one with his phone number on it?"

"The phone? Jesus. You think they're tracking it? I'm sorry, Nicole. This is on me. The phone's up in our apartment on the table by the door, along with the all access IDs for the employee-only areas of the airport."

"So we know how, but we don't know who. What do you want to do?"

"We could scoop up one of the sporting goods guys, but that's just going to show our hand. We need to get back into our apartment before we leave town, so we're just going to have to wait them out. In the meantime, we stick with the program. Aaron's place is probably a dead end. So we've got to find Eagle Tattoo, and get the casket back to the museum before the Feds get active. Who knows? Maybe Eagle Tattoo knows our guys."

"Okay," Nicole said. "Might as well set up in a corner booth here."

"You're reading my mind. Large coffee, good Internet connection to get some research done—got a lot of phone calls to make."

GRACE MOSLEY SAT at a computer monitor in the security center at the Charles Bay Freeport offices going through the video surveillance footage from last night, running the footage at triple speed. The security manager, a sandy-haired man with a jowly, retired-cop face, sat in the chair next to her, stroking his red-and-blue-striped necktie. "See? What did I tell you? Nothing on the main cameras. Caught two of them on the right loading dock camera behind Premium Security Transit, but they're wearing masks. I'm going to say it's the same two at the perimeter fence, but it's too far away to be sure."

"Anyone else have a look at these?"

"You're the first."

"Could you queue up the loading dock for me?"

She rolled her chair back. He reached in front of her to the keyboard, found the file, and opened it. She watched two grainy figures, a man and a woman, come out of the back door carrying a duffel bag, move out of the camera's sightline, and then reappear behind the utility vehicle. They drew their sidearms. Bullets rained in around them and ricocheted off the concrete wall behind them.

"That's some firepower."

"Got to be at least three shooters. Assault rifles, judging by the caliber."

The firing stopped. They moved out of the sightline again, and then the vehicle disappeared. "But there were no bodies?"

"None left. Detectives found blood. The truck was up the alley around the corner, all shot to hell. It's still being processed. Surprised you guys aren't in charge."

"Freeport is a Customs responsibility, so Homeland Security is running the show. We don't want to get involved if we don't have to."

The manager smiled. "Look, you don't have to spin me a story. We're happy to cooperate."

"Just trying to avoid a pissing contest."

"Fair enough."

Mosley stood up and grabbed the back of her chair to roll it up to the desk. "What's on the fence footage?"

"Two people moving along the fence that separates the freeport from the private airfield."

"But they're too far away to see clearly. They carrying anything?"

He shook his head. "Their hands are empty."

"Could you hang on to the loading dock and perimeter fence footage for me?"

"No problem."

"And I'd appreciate it if you'd keep this visit to yourself."

The manager stood up. "If nobody asks me, I won't tell them."

Mosley pushed out the double glass doors of the security office and walked across the parking lot to her car. Gray clouds were rolling in from over the ocean, piling up over the city. Would there be rain this afternoon or would the clouds blow off? She sat down in her car. Aaron didn't fake the theft of the Cellini casket. That was a real theft. She thought about the surveillance footage. The pair who'd brought out the bag didn't give up when they were outnumbered and ambushed. Judging from where the truck ended up, and how they'd been seen at the fence, they'd gone after the bag to retrieve it, but had been fought off and had then managed to escape. The guy Aaron met at the rest stop must have been in the crew that ended up with the casket. So either Aaron had been tipped off about the robbery and used the information to his advantage, or he had planned the robbery and set up the robbers. A risky opening move, but one that paid off by putting another set of people between him and the robbery.

Aaron wasn't thinking like a cop; he was thinking like a crook. From the very beginning of this sting operation, he was putting his job, his freedom, and his life on the line. He was even more reckless and unstable than she'd thought last night. What else had he lied about? What really was his relationship with Philips? Was the forged painting he sold Philips part of his investigation, or did he simply get caught being too smart for his own good? Was there even a sting operation at all? Or was Aaron just hatching a plan to screw over Philips and make some money? At this point, she couldn't tell. Either way, she had to make sure she stayed upwind of his problems. She wasn't going to do anything to jeopardize her extra income, and the farther Aaron ran down the rabbit hole, the harder he was going to be to help.

Mosley tapped her fingers on the steering wheel. If she was going to Nohamay City, she had to call Clare. She couldn't put it off any longer. She just didn't want to rehash the argument they had the last time they spoke. How could she avoid the topic? What was the best approach to smooth things over? Maybe if she just kept things simple. She took out her phone. "Clare? I'm glad I caught you, sweetie. I thought you might be at work."

"I haven't left yet."

"How have you been?"

"I haven't seen you in a while."

"I know. I've been busy. I miss you." There was a pause on the line.

"I miss you, too."

"The reason I called—I just wanted to let you know that I'm on my way to you. Be there in a day or two. Wanted to give you the heads up, you know, in case you had someone new."

"There's nobody new."

"Really? Can I stay over? I don't want to impose."

"Call me with your flight information."

"Can't wait to see you." She ended the call. That went better than expected. Clare dealt blackjack at the Great Circle Casino, but she was also Mosley's contact in Nohamay City. When Philips wanted something taken to his freeport vault locker, one of his men gave Mosley an aluminum attaché case—as a federal agent she could avoid airport security—and she flew into Nohamay City. She gave the case to Clare, who handed it off to the person authorized to enter the locker. The first time she met Clare, it was as if they were long-lost sisters, and within a few trips they were best buddies. Then one evening at Clare's condo, while they were sitting on the sofa watching a movie, Clare had leaned over and kissed her. Mosley knew Clare was a lesbian, had from the very beginning, and she suspected Clare's interest in her was more than platonic, so she hadn't been surprised that Clare would try to kiss her, but she had been surprised by her own response. She'd kissed her back. There was a softness in that kiss that she hadn't expected, a softness that felt at once warm and electric. They didn't sleep together that night, or even on the next trip. But eventually, as if it had always been meant to happen, they ended up in bed.

Mosley drove across the parking lot to the freeport gate. It would be great to see Clare again. She was wonderful to touch. The feminine closeness they shared was something that Mosley hadn't experienced anywhere else. She always looked forward to it. She wasn't in love with Clare, and she hadn't lied to her about it, and that's what led to their argument. But maybe everything was okay now. She really hoped so. On this trip, if she were going to stay in Philips's good graces and keep Aaron from getting killed, her visit to Nohamay City was going to be a lot more stressful than usual. She needed Clare's condo to be her island of peace.

By MIDAFTERNOON RON and Nicole had moved from the Caffeination coffee shop through a Taco Verde at lunchtime to a PourAway coffee shop at a strip mall off the beltway. Ron had spent the day calling people who didn't know Eagle Tattoo but who knew someone who might know him, dead ends piling up like dog-eared magazines at a dentist's office. "Thanks, Jimbo," he said.

Nicole looked up from across the table. "Any luck?"

"Just another lead." He dialed the new number.

"Palace Barbeque," the man's voice said.

"Mikey? Jimmy Stevens gave me your number, said you might be able to help me out."

"How's that?"

"You know a big guy, red beard, eagle tattoo on his hand?"

"Tommy? I know him a little. What you looking for him for?"

"Got some work he might be interested in. You got a number for him?"

"No, I don't. But a buddy of his comes in here most days after work."

"What's his name?"

"This isn't any bullshit, is it? I don't want to get anybody in trouble."

"I'm just trying to hire a reliable crew, if you know what I mean."

"Richie. Wears a biker jacket. Has a blue snake tattooed on his neck."

"Thanks a lot."

Ron ended the call and looked over at Nicole. "Find Palace Barbeque on the map."

They drove over to the near west side into a poor white neighborhood that surrounded two shut-down metal works plants. The Palace Barbeque was a narrow brick two-story building that could have been a bank once upon a time. It was located on a corner across from a boarded-up grocery store. It didn't smell as if there was any barbeque being cooked inside. They drove down the side of the building to the back parking lot and parked at the far back, next to the alley. The lot was crowded with old cars and work trucks, and a row of motorcycles was parked up next to the building. The back door was propped open with a concrete block. Honky-tonk music blasted out. While they sat there, a pair of longhaired men dressed in work clothes came out the back, got into a truck, sat for a few minutes, and then went back inside.

Ron leaned back in his seat. "Selling drugs in the parking lot. Not worried about the cops at all. We're not dressed for this venue. Everyone will remember us."

"You want me to bring the guy out?"

He shook his head. "He's probably one of Tommy's crew."

They got out of the car. Ron put on his suit coat to cover up the Smith & Wesson on his hip. As they walked across the gravel, an unshaven man wearing a biker jacket stumbled out the door with his arm around a drunken bleached blonde wearing a very short red dress. As he dug his sunglasses out of his shirt pocket, he turned. A blue snake was tattooed on his neck.

"Luck's changing," Nicole said.

"You better knock on wood," Ron replied. He hollered over at the man. "Richie!"

Richie turned, let go of the woman, and balled his hands into fists. "Who are you?"

"I'm looking for Tommy."

The woman pushed her hair out of her face, pulled a pack of cigarettes and a lighter out of her bra, and lit a cigarette. She squinted at Nicole as if she were sizing up the competition. "Let's go, baby."

"Tommy who?" Richie said.

Ron looked at Richie's sunglasses as if he could see his eyes. "Mikey told me you could hook me up. I'm trying to get a job done. Want to see if Tommy's interested."

"Mikey, huh?" Richie let his hands hang loose. "Why don't you tell me what you got in mind—save you the trouble of finding Tommy?"

One of the men who'd come out earlier came out the door with a different companion. They all glanced at him. He shepherded his friend around and went back inside. Ron looked back at Richie. "Busy place." He turned to Nicole. "What you think?"

She nodded.

He turned back to Richie. "Let's go somewhere a little quieter."

The drunken woman dropped her cigarette and crushed it out. "You come back when you're done. Maybe I'll still be here." She started back into the bar.

"Hold on, Sally." Richie looked at Ron. He grinned. "How about we meet a little later."

Ron shook his head. "Wish I could, but I'm on a timeline."

Richie looked at Sally, who was plucking at the hem of her dress, sighed, and turned back to Ron. "Let me give you Tommy's phone number."

AT 8:00 P.M., Ron and Nicole were driving down a street in an old neighborhood of little houses north of the shipping docks. Midblock was the house they were looking for—a peeling white clapboard with a full-length open porch and a three-foot-tall chain-link fence marking out the yard. A black Ford pickup truck was parked at the curb. The gate hung open. A pink girl's bike with training wheels stood on the sidewalk at the bottom of the steps. Inside, they could see Tommy Bartholomew, a.k.a. Eagle Tattoo, sitting in the living room with a blonde woman. A little blonde girl sat in his lap. Ron turned around at the end of the block and parked on the opposite side of the street four houses down. "Wife and kid," Nicole said.

"Houseful of complications. We're going to have to wait him out."

They sat watching the house. At 9:30 p.m., the lights went out in the living room, followed very shortly by the rest of the lights. Ron got out of the car and walked around the block to see what he could see of the back of the house. All dark. When he got back to the Cadillac, he sent Nicole to find coffee. He walked down to the bus stop and waited. He could hear a dog barking in the distance. An unshaven graybeard in an old blue Volvo drove slowly by. Ron put his hands in his pockets and shuffled from one foot to the other, as if he were tired of waiting. The Volvo turned right at the end of the block. A few minutes later Nicole pulled up at the bus stop. Ron climbed into the passenger's side. "What did you get?"

"Convenience store coffee was the best I could do. Brought you a package of cashews as a consolation."

"Thanks." Ron put the nuts in his shirt pocket.

Nicole pulled out from the bus stop, drove down the street, and pulled to the curb a few houses away from the Bartholomews'. "Ron," she said, "the casket has been in the wind twenty-four hours. Do you really think we still have a chance?"

"Yes, I do. If Bartholomew comes through for us, and we start after Aaron tomorrow, it's all still doable." He shrugged. "But every hour is against us. If we can't catch a break before tomorrow evening, we'll be entirely out of luck."

"You been thinking about our backup plan?"

"We've got some unknown bad guys watching our house. It's just a matter of time before the Feds start after us. If we can't make progress, we'll have to run hard and fast, maybe leave the country if we can get through an airport before the Feds get any pictures of us. And without any money—God, I hate working overseas. So many new variables. I hate working—or jailing—with people who don't speak English."

"We did okay in Mexico that one time."

"Yeah, you're right. There's always the resort traffic. The trick is always to do the best with what you've got. And that's what we're going to do. We have to. We've got no choice." He glanced down the street at the Bartholomews' house. "I think it's going to be a long night. You want first watch or second?"

"First."

"Okay." He leaned back into the corner of the seat and the door and closed his eyes.

4

NOHAMAY CITY

At 3:30 a.m., the lights came on inside the Bartholomews' house. Ron set down the cold coffee he'd been sipping and put his hand on Nicole's shoulder. "Wake up, honey."

She shifted around in the driver's seat and sat up. "Rain?"

"Started about an hour ago. Misting, mainly."

"And the lights are on?"

"You want any of this cold coffee?"

She shook her head. "Where do you want me?"

Ron got out his .38 revolver. "When he comes outside and heads for the truck, you're going to roll up to him, and I'm going to persuade him to help us."

"He's a big guy."

"Just don't let him get his truck door open."

"Don't accidentally kill him."

"Relax."

At 4:00 a.m., the house went dark, and Tommy Bartholomew came out onto the porch in boots, jeans and a gray sweatshirt with the sleeves cut off. The rain had stopped. He has a lunch pail in one hand. Nicole started the Cadillac and counted off Bartholomew's steps to get in sync with him. One, two, three, his boot was on the first step down from the porch. She pulled out of her parking spot. He walked around his daughter's bike. Nicole was two houses away, driving the speed limit. He glanced back toward them as he came around the back of his black truck. One house. He unlocked the truck door. Nicole turned the wheel. Bartholomew spun around just as the Cadillac slid in next to the truck, trapping him between the vehicles. Ron lowered his window and pointed his gun with both hands. "Don't struggle and you'll get out of this alive. You don't want your woman and your baby to find you dead in the street."

"Are you crazy? You're crushing me here."

"You sound like you've got plenty of breath."

"Who the hell are you?"

"You know us, Tommy. You ripped us off two days ago."

"You've got the wrong guy."

"Bullshit. You need to start wearing gloves on the job or get that eagle tat removed."

Bartholomew glanced at his house. The lights were still off. "What do you want?"

"We want our money and the crate."

Bartholomew shook his head. "Too late. The crate is gone."

"Where did it go?"

"I don't know. Our guy got on a plane right after I gave it to him. That's all I know."

"Where's the money?"

"Don't have it yet. We get paid after the sale."

Ron pushed the barrel of the pistol into Bartholomew's chest. "Right here. This is where you'll be dead. You won't even hear the ambulance. Memories for your family to last a lifetime."

"That's the truth. I don't know why you're so pissed. It was business. I lost two guys, and you two are barely scratched."

Ron held up a photo of Rickover. "This your guy?"

Bartholomew nodded. "That's him."

"Keep your mouth shut if you want to keep holding your little girl." He turned to Nicole. "Let's go."

Nicole swung out away from the truck. Ron watched out his

window as Bartholomew leaned back against the door, his lunch pail hanging at his side, and reached into his back pocket. His hand came up clutching a pack of cigarettes. Nicole turned right at the corner. "So Aaron flew out of here. Must have had a buyer already set up."

"That's Aaron. Always trying to play one step out. Right now I'm just glad I didn't ditch the airport IDs."

Nicole smiled. "I see where you're going." She turned left, working her way east toward Field Boulevard heading downtown. "If Aaron took a red-eye, he's on the surveillance cameras. We just have to follow him from security to his gate."

"Exactly. We've got to slip back into the airport. It's a risk, but it's one we've got to take. Let's drive by our place. See if it's safe to pick up the IDs."

BARTHOLOMEW SAT in his truck and caught his breath. Who were those crazy motherfuckers that Aaron set them on? He pressed on his ribs. They hurt, but they didn't feel broken. Those two were outgunned and outmanned. They should have been moving on, nursing their wounds, looking for an easier job, instead they were all about payback. He shook his right foot. It felt like it had been run over, but he could wiggle his toes. He had to get to work. He was supposed to make an early start on the third-floor framing. He started his truck and pulled out. Goddamn Aaron Rickover. He wasn't going to do any more jobs for him. As soon as he got his cut for this job, he was done.

He pulled through a PourAway coffee shop drive-through on his way to the job site and bought a large coffee. He sipped it as he drove. It was hot and bitter, but as he drank it down he began to feel better. The dark was just beginning to lift as he parked on the street a block from the half-bricked exterior of the apartment building where he was doing rough-in interior carpentry. As he got out of his truck with his hardhat and his lunch pail, four men rushed up to him, two black and two white, all wearing chinos with golf shirts and black nylon jackets.

One of the black men, clean-shaven and neatly barbered, obviously the leader, gave Bartholomew an appraising look. "You Tommy Bartholomew?"

Bartholomew looked at him sharply. "I know you?"

"You're coming with us."

His hardhat and lunch pail clattered to the pavement as he balled up his left fist and dug into his right back pocket for his lock-back knife.

The other black man, a tall, thin man sporting a goatee, grabbed Bartholomew's left arm. The closer white man, a heavily muscled guy with a blond crew cut, grabbed his right. The other white man, messy brown hair and a beer belly, pulled an automatic pistol from his pocket. "Easy or hard," the leader said, "easy or hard."

"Okay, okay," Bartholomew said. "What's this about?"

The leader smiled. "We work for Mr. Philips. I'm sure you know who he is. We just need to have a little chat."

A green Suburban pulled up, and they piled Bartholomew into the middle of the backseat.

RON AND NICOLE rolled slowly down their street, looking for anyone who might be watching their apartment. The streetlights were still the only real light. Most of the apartments were dark. The cars parked on both sides of the street were empty. Nicole turned into the alley next to their building. Ron got out. She continued down the alley to the next street.

Ron used his key at the back door, padded quietly up the hall to the front, and stopped at the doorway to the front entry. All he could hear was his own breathing. He slowly stuck his head around the corner. There was no one there. He hurried up the stairs to the second floor and repeated the process. The hall to their apartment door was clear. He put his ear up against the door, straining to hear any sound at all, but he heard nothing. He put his key in the lock, turned it, and then carefully eased the door open.

The living room was empty. The phone and the airport IDs were still on the side table by the door. He scooped them into his pockets and hurried back down the stairs and out the back. The night was dissipating, and the birds were beginning to chirp. He walked down the alley along a row of dumpsters, pulled the chip from the burner phone, tossed it and the phone into the closest dumpster, and continued to the next street, where he waited until he saw their Cadillac appear around the corner. He waved. Nicole stopped in the street, and he hopped into the car.

"I got the IDs."

"What about the phone?"

"Trashed it."

PHILIPS'S MEN drove Bartholomew to the construction site of the new uptown parking ramp. Mitch, the white guy with the beer belly, hopped out and unlocked the chain-link gate. They continued onto the new concrete of the parking deck and drove down to the basement level, where the plywood forms were set to pour the footing for a stairwell. Jacob, the guy with the blond crew cut, and Charles, the black man with the goatee, pulled Bartholomew from the truck and pushed him over to the footing hole. "What the hell?" Bartholomew yelled.

Mitch and Jermaine, a heavy-set black man wearing black-framed glasses, joined Jacob and Charles, each grabbing hold of Bartholomew's arms and shoulders. Gary, the leader, pointed down into the hole at the cement-stained plywood and rusty rebar. "Unless you want this to be your final resting place, you're going to answer my questions. You're going to tell the truth. Where did Aaron Rickover go?"

"I don't know."

"They're pouring concrete here in two hours."

"He didn't tell me. He never does."

"No one will find you." The men gripping Bartholomew leaned him over the hole. He bucked and strained, but they held him tight.

Gary continued. "You'll be under the slab. Your woman and your kid will think you ran off."

Bartholomew turned his head to look up at Gary. "You think I'd cover for Rickover? He's caused me nothing but trouble. I don't know where he is. I'd tell you if I did."

Gary stepped up close enough to feel Bartholomew's breath on his face. "They'll think you never loved them. They'll remember you as the bastard who left them with a pile of bills and no money. Didn't even say goodbye."

"I don't know. I'm telling you, I don't know where he went."

Gary looked hard in Bartholomew's eyes. "You know, I think I believe you." He turned to Jacob. "We're done here."

Jacob patted Bartholomew on the shoulder and smiled. "See how easy that was?" Before Bartholomew could reply, he slipped a wire loop over Bartholomew's head and pulled it tight around his neck. Bartholomew struggled and kicked, but the others forced him to his knees. Gary turned away. He took out his phone as he walked back to the Suburban. "Marty? Tell the boss that the redneck didn't know anything, and we're cleaning up as we go."

RON AND NICOLE walked down a deserted hallway in the "employee only" area of the airport. The first set of early morning flights would be boarding soon, but the day staff wouldn't be in the airport for a few more hours. The building plans showed a suite of manager offices just up the hall. Ron punched in the access code and opened the door.

"Who are you?" A blue-uniformed custodian pushing a cleaning cart stood directly in front of them. He was wiry-looking black man with close-cropped gray hair.

"Security consultants." Ron said. "Who are you?"

"This is my floor. This one and the two below. Nobody told me about any consultants."

"Wouldn't be a surprise if everyone had a chance to put away all the stuff they're not supposed to leave out, would it?"

"Doesn't seem right to me."

Ron pointed to the ID clipped on his jacket. "Would we have these full-access credentials if we weren't supposed to be here?"

The custodian glanced at the ID and then at Ron. "You're right. That makes sense. Not trying to cause trouble."

"I understand. You're just trying to do your job. Make sure there's no unauthorized people inside the security envelope."

Ron and Nicole stepped around the cart and into the room, which contained four cubicles, all in a row along the windows. Then they split up, each examining the desktops as if looking for security breaches. The custodian pushed his cart out of the office. The door closed behind him. Nicole slipped up to the door, turned the handle slowly, and then cracked the door open, being careful not to make a sound. She watched the custodian push his cart down the hall to another door on the opposite side of the hallway, punch in an access code, and push his cart in. She turned to Ron. "All clear."

They put on latex gloves and started going through the desks, looking for computer passwords. On a post-it in a pencil tray, Ron found a likely candidate, a sequence of ten letters and numbers. He turned on the computer. Nicole came over to watch. He keyed in the sequence on the password page. Nothing. He opened the side drawers: a stapler, file folders, bits of junk. A paperweight of a snowman that looked like it was made in an elementary school art class sat on the corner of the desk. Nicole picked it up. A post-it was stuck to the bottom. Another sequence of numbers and letters. Ron keyed it in. The home page appeared.

Ron stood up and Nicole sat down. She clicked on the security icon from the row at the bottom of the screen, chose "surveillance" from the menu, the date of the robbery, and started looking at footage from the TSA screening point starting at 10:00 p.m. Passengers trickled through. At 10:32 p.m., Aaron Rickover appeared. He walked right through the scanner. No carry-on luggage. He walked out of range. Nicole switched to the next camera. A few frames later, he turned up again. She followed him down the hallways, camera by camera, past a coffee shop, in and out of a men's room, into a knickknack shop where he bought a bottle of water, and down to gate C 31, where boarding was already in progress. She opened another screen to check the scheduled departures. Nohamay Nation Holiday Getaway.

She looked at Ron. "Good or bad?"

He shrugged. "Casino, I think. Google them up."

She opened a new window, typed in "Nohamay Casino," and clicked on the link. "Here we go," she said. They read the entry.

"Jesus," Ron said. "Nohamay City. Casino, alternative medicine hospital, and freeport. Bet they're making bank. Upside, the place is run by the NewTrust Corporation, so it's probably all private security. Downside, the freeport vault is in a tunnel cut into the side of a mesa. It was originally going to be a nuclear waste dump, so its power grid is isolated. If the casket is in there, it will be hell getting it out. Click on the map."

She pulled up the map of the city. He pointed at the screen. "There's only one road out. So it's fly or drive across the desert."

"But is he still there, or was he just using it for a connecting flight?"

"I guess we're going to find out."

"We could still give up and run."

"I'm not running empty-handed. Aaron is out there with our money. He's just not that smart. Besides, I think we can still return the casket and get in the clear. The odds are moving against us, but we've still got some time. We just need our breaks to come a little faster."

It was daylight by the time they got back to their neighborhood. They circled the block slowly, twice, looking for the men wearing the chinos and golf shirts or for anyone else who didn't belong. There were the usual neighbors waiting at the bus stop—moms and dads waiting with kids for the school bus, a painter's van in front of the building that was being remodeled, but no strangers. "I wonder why they're gone. Maybe they weren't here for us," Nicole said.

"If not us, then who? All the neighbors are squeaky clean. And they looked like they belonged to the same crew as the two guys watching Aaron's apartment." Ron pulled into an empty spot on the street between a Prius and old Ford Focus. "I admire your optimism, but let's not take any chances. Let's pack and get out of here. No dawdling, no showers."

They went up into their apartment. Ron unlocked the door and pushed it open slowly. The living room was empty. Sunlight washed into the kitchenette through the windows that faced the street. He turned on the lights. Everything appeared to be just as it was when they left yesterday. Two coffee cups sat on the counter over the dishwasher. Old newspapers lay on the glass-topped coffee table next to the TV remote. A pair of Nicole's high heels lay just to the right of the doorway to the hall where she had kicked them off. They went into their bedroom, pulled carry-on suitcases from the closet shelf, and started packing a week's worth of clothes, as if they were going on an upscale vacation. While Ron was in the bathroom collecting his shaving kit, the doorbell rang. "Nicole."

She came out of the bedroom and stood waiting in the hall. Ron looked out the peephole in the front door. "Who is it?"

A police badge filled his line of vision. "Police. Can we have a word with you?"

Ron opened the door. Two middle-aged men in suits stood in the hallway. One wore an old-school flattop haircut and steel-rim glasses. He was clipping his badge back on his belt. "What's this about?" Ron asked.

The other cop was a Latino with dark, gray-streaked hair and a cleft chin. "Can we come in? There's no reason to tell your business to the neighbors."

Ron shrugged and motioned them in. Nicole stepped in from the hall to the bedroom. The cop with the glasses said, "Is there anyone else here?"

"No," Ron said.

Nicole smiled. "Would you like to sit down? Can I get you a glass of water or a cup of coffee?"

"We're fine," the Latino said.

"So why are you here?" Ron asked.

"Do you own a gun, Mr. Sherman?" the Latino continued.

"Do you have a valid carry permit?" the other cop asked.

"Let me show you." Ron took out his wallet and handed the Latino cop a concealed carry permit in the name of Martin Sherman. The cop examined it carefully.

"Do you have another form of ID?"

Ron handed him a driver's license in the name of Martin Sherman. "So what is this about?"

"A man accused you of threatening him with a gun at the Deal's Motel."

Ron opened his mouth to speak, but the other cop cut him off. "It's on the motel cameras."

Ron continued. "Then you saw that lecher threatened my wife. He was outside in his underwear, grabbed at her. He was acting crazy."

The cop wearing the glasses smiled. "We saw what we saw. Everybody's got a storyline to go with the pictures. Bottom line: stay away from that man. We're not putting up with any stand-your-ground bullshit. You've been warned."

The Latino cop nodded. "We're watching you."

"We done here?"

The Latino cop handed Ron the driver's license and the carry permit. "Don't screw this up, Mr. Sherman. You don't want us looking into you."

The cops left. Ron locked the door behind them. "The nerve of that bastard. Calling the cops on us after what he did."

"They sure found us fast."

"They just wanted us to know they could bring pressure to bear. McCall must have picked me out from the concealed-carry database."

"At least now we know the permit is still good."

"Zeb is always reliable when it comes to documents."

"Which guns are registered to Sherman?"

"The two Glocks and the Smith & Wesson .38. Guess I'll be buying airline tickets as Martin Sherman. Hard to buy guns on the street in a controlled environment like Nohamay City. They'll have to travel in checked baggage, but at least we'll have them when we get there."

They started walking back toward the bedroom. "How much longer to pack?" he asked.

"Maybe ten minutes."

"Me too. Still got to get my shaving kit and another pair of shoes. And I'm grabbing all the passports, just in case."

AT 10:00 A.M., Aaron Rickover stood at a marble-topped counter in a viewing room in the Nohamay Mountain Vault, located in the freeport at Nohamay City. His hands were sweaty, and his wire-rim glasses didn't seem to want to stay up on his nose. Across from him stood James Denison, a trust-fund millionaire. He was tall and thin with short gray hair and a tightly trimmed beard. He wore snake-skin cowboy boots, dark blue jeans, and a red golf shirt under a white linen sports coat. The Cellini casket sat on the counter between them.

"This is really beautiful," Denison said.

Rickover pointed with the eraser end of a pencil at the edges of the lid and the box. "Look at the quality of these engravings. Imagine: he did this work freehand with only rudimentary magnification."

Denison pointed at a cluster of indentations on the top. "Looks like there used to be jewels here."

"According to the Gould and Sons 1863 description, there were three large white pearls and two rubies. They were removed sometime before World War One." Rickover looked up at Denison. "Does it meet your expectations?"

"This is definitely a Cellini?"

"As I told you, Mr. Denison, there used to be some question of authenticity, as there often is in these cases, but the consensus of the top scholars says yes."

Denison smiled. "My wife will love it."

"So it's a deal?"

"I just don't understand how it can be so—."

"Inexpensive?"

"Yeah. Cellini's salt cellar, which is about this size, is way out of my reach."

Rickover smiled. This was where he had to choose his words carefully. "That's a special piece with a special history. And it's not for sale. As I explained on the phone, the current owner of the casket doesn't want anyone to know that they had to sell. That's why you had to stipulate that you would keep this sale quiet. What can I say? It's a vanity thing. If this jewelry casket went to auction, it would probably get more than one and a half million."

"So I give you one hundred thousand as a down payment, and I can keep the casket in my locker until I have a chance to show it to my wife?"

"Absolutely. You just can't remove it from this facility."

"It may be a while."

"No problem. So long as you can come to a decision in the next two weeks."

Denison pushed a brown accordion envelope across the marble counter. "You specified cash, right?"

"Thank you, Mr. Denison." Rickover's hands were shaking. He glanced at the bundles of hundred-dollar bills in the envelope and then tucked the envelope into his briefcase. "I'll leave you with it."

Rickover closed the door as he left the viewing room. The lobby had marble walls and plush carpeting, although the twelve-foot ceiling still bore excavation scars and was reinforced by roof bolts. The only natural light that entered the space poured in through the front wall, which was bulletproof glass. He hurried across the lobby, glancing nonchalantly at the business representatives sitting at their desks dealing with clients, and pushed out the heavy glass doors on the other side of the security scanners.

Outside, beyond the parking lot, the scrub desert continued uninterrupted all the way back to the low, brown mountains in the distance. The day was already oppressively hot. He mopped his face with his handkerchief. Now that he had Denison's $100,000, nothing could stop him. He'd give the money to Philips, have Grace arrest him for involvement in art theft, get the warrant to search Philips's locker, and voila, he'd get his promotion. There would be no one to contradict his story about how the theft of the casket took place. He patted the bulge of the accordion envelope in his briefcase and smiled to himself. It was just a matter of days now. He'd show them all what he was capable of—his ex, Philips, his bosses, even Grace. None of them would ever underestimate him again.

THAT AFTERNOON, after Mosley checked into her cover-story room at the Great Circle Casino and Convention Center in Nohamay City and hung her FBI clothes in the closet, she took a taxi to a row of stucco one-story condos in a residential area five blocks away. The taxi driver set her carry-on bag on the curb. She pulled out the telescoping handle on her bag and rolled it up the short sidewalk to a nearby front door. She opened the door with a key and lifted her bag over the threshold. A busty blonde in her midthirties, softly round in her hips and shoulders, her long hair held back in a loose ponytail, looked up from the cooktop built into the granite-topped island of the kitchenette.

Mosley smiled. "Miss me, Clare?"

Clare came around the island. She was wearing sandals, faded jeans, and a pink cotton cardigan sweater whose sleeves were pushed up her forearms. "You should have called. I would have met you at the airport."

"I wanted to surprise you."

They met in the middle of the living room between the sofa and the flat-screen TV, held each other for a moment, and kissed. Mosley continued, "You wanted me to come back, didn't you?"

"Of course. Everything is fine between us, Grace. I'm just not good with surprises. How was your flight?"

"I just wanted to be sure. The way we left it—"

She nodded. "I understand. You felt I was rushing things."

"So you're okay with where I'm at? I want to be with you. I think you're wonderful, but I'm just not ready to say you're my only one. Are you really okay? 'Cause I could get a hotel."

"As long as you're not saying that our relationship can't grow."

"I'm not saying that. I'm definitely not saying that."

Clare smiled, took Mosley's hands, and kissed her again. "Then you should definitely stay here."

"Great. Glad we made it through that." Mosley stepped out of her shoes. "This run is a little different from usual. I'm not making a drop. Might be here a few days. What smells so good?"

"I'm making lasagna."

"Enough for two?"

"There'll be plenty."

"I can't wait. How have you been?"

"The same." She motioned toward the kitchen. "I've got to keep moving."

Mosley followed her. "The same?"

Clare cracked open the oven door and peeked inside. "I've picked up a few evening shifts. Better tips."

"Great. The boss sends his best." Mosley got a bottle of beer from the refrigerator. "You want one?"

Clare shook her head. "Not yet. After I make the salad." She looked into a pot on the stove and gave it a stir. "So if you're not making a drop, what are you doing?"

Mosley shook her head. "Can't say."

Clare turned to look at her, the wooden spoon still in her hand.

"Trust me," Mosley said. "You're better off not knowing."

It was dark when Philips's Gulfstream 200 taxied to a stop outside the Crenshaw Industries airplane hangar at the private airfield next to the Nohamay City Airport. Inside were the same men who had murdered Bartholomew at the parking ramp construction site that morning. Their leader, Gary, the black man with the neatly trimmed hair, stood up in the aisle at the front of the plane facing the rest of them, the top of his head just shy of the ceiling height.

"Okay, guys, this is what's going to happen. Rickover is here somewhere. We're going to find him and collect the boss's money. We're going to do this so quietly that the locals won't even know we're here. So no fucking around. No drinking, no gambling, no whores. Not even part-timers. The locals can be a pain in the ass, and the boss has business here he doesn't want interrupted. Everybody understand?"

They all nodded.

He continued. "The casino has metal detectors. We can't take weapons in there, so we're going to work out of the airplane hangar. Leave our gear here when we can't be carrying. Two teams. Black and white. Blend in and get it done. Questions?"

Jacob, the blond bodybuilder, rubbed his crew cut and yawned. "This Rickover guy. How gentle do we have to be?"

"We get the money first. Then we clean up the mess. Let me repeat. The boss wants his money. He's going to be extremely pissed if Rickover dies first."

"Got you."

Gary looked at the others. "Anybody else?" No one spoke. He pressed a button by the door to the cockpit. The pilot, a gray man in a crumpled dark blue uniform, came out and opened the plane's door and lowered the steps. Gary looked over his shoulder at Mitch, the dark-haired guy with the potbelly. "You and Jacob grab the foot locker." Then he turned to the pilot. "Keep your phone on, Tony."

"I'll be ready."

They all hurried down the steps and went into the airplane hangar, Jacob and Mitch lugging a heavy, black footlocker between them. The tarmac was quiet. The overhead doors to the hangar were up, revealing an office space to one side. Jacob and Mitch set the footlocker down next to a folding table. Gary unlocked it. Inside were handguns packed in their cases and boxes of ammunition. He looked over at Jermaine, the large black man, who was wiping his glasses with the corner of his shirt. "You're with Mitch. You two are scouting around town, so you may as well arm up."

"Sweet," Jermaine replied.

Gary turned to Charles, the skinny black man with the goatee, and Jacob. "You two are checking out the casino."

Jacob frowned. Mitch chuckled. "What's a matter? Thought a big guy like you didn't need a gun."

"You could trade with me," Jacob said.

Mitch snorted. "Not a chance."

AT 11:05 P.M., the last plane of the day landed at the Nohamay City Airport. Ron and Nicole, still dressed in the wrinkly city clothes they'd been wearing for over thirty-six hours, walked into the gate and down the hallway to the baggage claim area. They stood among the other arriving passengers, who were all dressed in their festive vacation clothes—sleeveless pastels, linen jackets, light-colored pants —and tried to blend in while they waited for their bags to come out on the baggage carousel. The bell sounded, the carousel turned, and their bags popped out among the others.

"So far, so good," Ron said.

They rolled their bags out onto the sidewalk in front of the airport. The night sky was bright with stars. The cool breeze felt good after the long plane ride. Across the boulevard, yellow and red lights flashed from the signs over the Rising Rapids Waterpark. The breeze shifted, and they could hear the sounds of rushing water and laughter. They got in a yellow cab in front of the airport for the four-block ride to the Arrowhead Hotel, a high rise, value hotel, which didn't have a policy against firearms, located next door to the Great Circle Casino and Convention Center.

There was no line at the lobby counter. They checked in using their Martin Sherman credit card, and the young Native American man behind the counter, wearing a red sweater vest with a green arrowhead logo on the chest, gave them a room on the twelfth floor. Their room had two queen beds and a view of the surrounding desert. They put their suitcases on the closest bed. Nicole lay down on the bed by the windows. Ron looked in all the drawers—empty— and the well-stocked refrigerator.

"Looks clean," he said.

He opened his suitcase, got out the locked gun cases and opened them. "Everything is here. Let's go over to the casino and get the lay of the land."

"I'm beat," Nicole said.

"The clock is ticking. That jewelry box isn't going to find itself."

"I'm going to shower and change first. You should too."

She got her shower bag from her suitcase and went into the bathroom, leaving the door open. Ron found his shaving kit, hung up his suit, left his shirt and underwear in a pile on the bed, and followed her into the bathroom. He shaved while she showered. She got out of the shower without turning off the water, and he traded places with her. When he got out of the shower, she was already out of the bathroom. He grabbed a towel from the stack over the towel rack. "A shower was a great idea."

She stuck her head in. "I feel better, but I look like death. I need about fourteen hours' sleep."

"You look great, honey—just like always."

She gave him a quick kiss. "Liar."

By the time he hung up his towel, she was back in the bathroom, dressed in dark green pants and a lightweight flower-print sweater with her makeup bag in her hand. "I'm almost ready," she said.

He put on khaki pants, a red golf shirt, and a blue blazer. Then he took the guns from their cases and locked them and the ammunition in the room safe in the corner of the closet. When he looked up, Nicole was standing beside him.

"Usual combination?" she asked.

"Always."

They went down the elevator and out the lobby. Even though it was near midnight, lots of people were on the street. They walked in the hotel entry to the Great Circle Casino and Convention Center. There was an Indian on horseback sculpture at the center of a fountain in the circle driveway. The huge lobby was furnished with sofas and easy chairs arranged in groups. Four-foot-tall cactuses in ceramic pots created screens to make the furniture arrangements more intimate. Across the back was a long reception counter where several people were standing in line to check in. To the left and right of the counter were hallways that led to the elevator clusters. On the left side of the lobby were a coffee shop and the entrance to a restaurant.

They took the front hallway to the casino. Tasteful signs indicated that no weapons were allowed. Just ahead of them was a short line at the security station where everyone had to pass through metal detectors. A few minutes later they were inside a large, dimly lit room filled with slot machines. A cacophony of machine and human noise gave the impression that every conversation was somehow private. They walked over to an area that was elevated a few steps so that they could improve their view. "Poker and blackjack are back there," Ron said.

Nicole nodded. "And there's a couple of bars with built-in slot machines."

Servers dressed in white-fringed black bikini tops and tight black pants moved through the crowds carrying drinks on trays.

"This is supposed to be an Indian casino, isn't it?" Ron asked.

"That's the idea."

"I wish there were more Indians and Asians in here. It would make it easier to spot Aaron."

They looked up and down the rows of slot machines as they moved toward the back of the room. They saw several bald, gray white men in glasses and cheap sports coats, but they were never Rickover. There were lots of people at the first group of blackjack tables, playing and watching, but Ron and Nicole weren't interested in games. Ron put his hand on Nicole's arm. "Get a drink?"

"Why not?"

They wandered over to the nearest bar and ordered two beers. They watched the people drift by, shoulders back and chest out, or slouching and foot dragging, depending on their wins or losses. Ron shook his head. "A whole building full of suckers. All ripe for the taking. Makes it hard to stay focused."

"Wait, wait, wait," Nicole said. "What about the guy in the hat coming out of the poker room?"

Ron tried to follow Nicole's look. "Which guy? Orient me."

"Far left, just walking by the first pillar, bald guy fedora."

"Got to have a closer look." He got off his stool.

There was a voice from behind them. "Hold up."

Ron and Nicole turned. A Native American with close-cropped hair and a burn scar on his left cheek, dressed in a charcoal gray pinstripe suit, stood behind them with two beefy, blue-uniformed security guards. "We need to talk with you."

"Who are you?" Ron asked.

"I'm Jason Stands-Alone, the casino general manager."

"What's this about?"

"Come with me."

The security guards stepped in close to Ron and Nicole, their hands resting on their gun butts and the pepper spray holstered at their waists. Stands-Alone led them through an employee-only door into a nondescript hallway and then into an office that was empty except for four chairs and a desk with a computer on it. Stands-Alone sat down at the desk, input a password on the computer, and began clicking through pictures. "Here you are," he said, swiveling the computer screen toward them. On the screen was a picture of Ron and Nicole from several years ago, captioned with the names Philip Rose and Tracy Benet. "You two are on the 'no gambling' database."

"We weren't gambling," Ron said.

"I know. We've been watching you since you came into the casino."

"So?"

"Just wanting to make sure you know how things stand."

Ron nodded. "So how do we stand?"

"You're welcome to look around, eat in the restaurants, see the shows, but if you try to gamble here, you'll be taking a one-way ride into the desert."

"We're not going to do any gambling."

The security guard closest to Ron gave him a push.

Stands-Alone continued. "There will be no second warning. We've seen every kind of disguise and ploy you professional hustlers use. We always catch you."

"Not doing any gambling."

"Then Bob and Jim here won't have to rough you up to convince you of our sincerity. Enjoy your stay in Nohamay City." He turned to the security guard closest to the door. "Take them back out on the floor."

The security guards walked them back down the hall and out into the casino. As soon as the security guards were gone, Ron took Nicole by the elbow and started steering her back toward the bar. "Assholes. Got nothing better to do. Let's see if we can catch up to that guy you saw."

They wove their way through the knots of gamblers, moving as fast as they could without being suspicious. Ron spotted a gray fedora bobbing in the crowd by the entrance to a restaurant. "Is that the guy?"

"Wrong color. The guy who might be Aaron was wearing a brown hat."

"What about that guy? No hat, but he looks like Aaron from behind."

"Over there." Nicole put her hand on Ron's shoulder. Through a break in the traffic, they saw Rickover on the other side of the room. Two men, a thin black man with a goatee and a bulked-up white man with a blond crew cut, were leading Rickover by the elbows. Ron and Nicole followed after them. They watched from behind a pillar as the two men took Rickover down a hallway that led to an exit door.

"Were those two of the sporting goods guys?"

"Don't know."

"We're not going to be able to take Rickover without our guns," Nicole said.

"Let's see where they're going."

"I'll tail them. You go for the guns. I'll text you."

He shook his head. "We need to stay together. We don't know who those guys are or how they're connected to Aaron."

They hurried down the hallway and stopped at the door. Nicole peeked out onto the street, which was brightly lit by streetlamps. The men were leading Rickover toward the waterpark. Ron and Nicole followed about a half block behind. "They aren't checking for tails at all," Nicole said.

"And Aaron isn't dragging his feet."

The waterpark was closing. The last few customers were trickling out—teenagers with their towels wrapped around their waists and parents leading cranky, wet children. At the crosswalk in front of the waterpark, Rickover and the two men crossed over to the airport side of the boulevard. The airport was closed, and the taxis were gone. The sidewalk was deserted.

Ron and Nicole stayed on the waterpark side of the boulevard, trailing along, still half a block behind. Rickover and the two men continued down the sidewalk, walking next to the chain-link fence that protected the airport, until they came to the entrance to the private airfield, where warehouses ran from the fence down to the airplane hangars that lined the tarmac. They disappeared into the darkness between two rows of warehouses. Ron and Nicole ran across the boulevard and followed them through the gate. Rickover and the men were nowhere in sight. Ron and Nicole stepped into the deep shadow of the nearest building.

"We need our guns," Nicole said.

"And daylight. I can't see a thing. The streetlights here are spaced too far apart. We can't risk being scooped up trying to find out which building they're in."

"What if they kill him?"

"Aaron isn't acting as if he's afraid. They could be his partners. If they aren't, and they do kill him, there's nothing we can do about it. We're running on fumes. We don't know what's really going on. We can't afford to make any mistakes now. We know he's here. The smart move is to wait until morning and pull a plan together."

5

THE FBI

The next morning, Ron and Nicole sat in a coffee shop, eating eggs and toast and drinking coffee. Neither was talking. Ron watched the servers move among the tables in their T-shirts and jeans, their aprons the only indicator of their employment, and thought about Rickover and the two men who were walking with him. Ron and Nicole were carrying their guns today. She had a Glock in her handbag, and he had the other one in a holster at the small of his back under his blue blazer and the Smith & Wesson in an ankle holster. Nicole was reading the *Charles Bay Tribune* on her smartphone, looking for more information about the investigation of the theft. Their server, a skinny twenty-something man with a porn-star mustache, came by with the coffee pot. Nicole flashed him a smile.

"Whoa," she said, glancing across the table at Ron. "Somebody caught up with Bartholomew."

"What's it say?"

"Man found murdered at new parking garage. Blah, blah, blah, Tommy Bartholomew, thirty-one, construction worker, blah, blah, found at eight a.m. when workers were adjusting the rebar for a concrete pour at the bottom of a stairwell. Gang task force has been assigned the case."

Ron sipped his coffee. "Okay. Think about the timeline. He was going to work when we left him. He must have been killed in the next couple of hours."

"Think about his wife and kid."

Ron shrugged. "He chose this life. What I'm saying is they killed him yesterday morning, and they scooped up Aaron in the evening. If they're already taking out the trash, we're probably too late."

"If they were the same crew—we don't know if it was the sporting goods guys—and if they scooped Aaron up, maybe they're his partners. Maybe they were watching our apartment as a favor to him. Last night, they weren't pushing him. He wasn't trying to slow them down."

Ron signaled for their check. "All true. We don't know what Aaron's situation really is. What we do know is that these guys will get ahead of us if we're not careful, and we still need Aaron if we're going to get the casket back." He tapped his fingers on the table. "So as much as I'd rather not do it, we're going to have to go looking in those warehouses."

They walked across the boulevard to the airport. The sun was already beating down, and the breeze was like a convection oven. People were hurrying in and out of the main doors, dragging luggage, looking for taxis or the baggage-check kiosk. Ron and Nicole ignored them. They traced their path down the sidewalk along the chain-link fence, past the runways to the private airfield gate. They stopped in the shadow of the first warehouse inside the airfield. It was a thirty-foot-tall, rust-red, corrugated steel building. Ron looked in the nearest dirt-encrusted window. Boxes stacked on pallets were arranged in the center of the space.

He turned to Nicole. "This is where we were. We saw Aaron come in the gate; we crossed; we came to here and stopped. We didn't see him or the two guys after they came in the gate."

Nicole nodded.

"How far behind him were we? Twenty seconds? Thirty seconds? Couldn't have been much more. It was dark. Too dark to chance without weapons. But there's a great sightline. The streets run straight down to the tarmac, and we didn't see anyone."

"So they must have gone into one of the nearby buildings."

"That's what I think."

"Could have left by now."

"Got to start somewhere. Let's check these four buildings nearest the gate first."

They walked around to the other side of the warehouse and looked in the windows. The view was the same as the first side. Boxes on pallets. They went to the next building. There was an extra-tall garage door in the side. They looked in the windows. Shipping containers on wheels sat in closely spaced rows. It was the same in the other two warehouses. They moved on to the next set. Nothing but boxes and containers.

They heard a door slam. A black man wearing khakis and a green golf shirt was walking away from a white-painted warehouse near the tarmac. Ron and Nicole ducked around the corner of a building. Nicole put her hand on Ron's arm. "Wasn't that one of the guys who was watching Aaron's apartment?"

"I didn't get a good look." Ron peeked around the corner. "The guy's gone. Let's get a look in that building."

They strolled down the street as if they were going to their own building nearby. "Crenshaw Industries" was painted in black lettering on the side. They glanced casually up at the rooflines of the surrounding buildings. There were no surveillance cameras. There was no one on the street, standing in a doorway, or peeking from behind a corner. They looked in the window in the door. Pallets of boxes stacked eight feet high stood in the center of the room. They couldn't see anyone. Ron turned the doorknob very slowly. The door was unlocked. He eased the door open enough to squeeze through and then held it open for Nicole. They could hear indistinct voices. They crept along the pallets of boxes, moving toward the voices, straining their ears to listen. Nicole had her hand on the Glock in her handbag.

Finally they could hear Rickover speaking. "How many times do I have to tell you? The money's gone. Lawyers, child support, the stock market swallowed it up. I'm broke."

A voice they didn't know replied. "Everybody's got something. In my experience, if I push hard enough, they remember. Before you leave here, I'm going to have the money you owe."

Another voice said, "What about the package? You think we didn't know about that? You came here with a package, met a guy at the vault."

Rickover said, "The package is gone. The only person I'm giving anything to is Mr. Philips. I've got to have his word that our business is settled."

The first voice said, "You're going to give us the money."

Rickover replied, "The only reason I'm still alive is that you don't have the money. I made a deal with your boss. He's the only guy I'll deal with."

The first voice said, "I think you need some time to think on this."

Ron and Nicole heard noise that sounded like a metal door opening and closing, and then footsteps growing louder. They slipped into a gap between two pallets and then turned into an open space among the boxes. A new voice said, "Where do you want to go to lunch?"

The first voice said, "Charles's picking something up."

The second voice said, "You calling the boss?"

The first voice said, "I'm not bothering him yet. We'll let this guy stew for a few hours in that sweat box, and then we'll see where we're at."

Ron and Nicole heard the door slam. They crept out of their hiding place and then peeked out of the gap between the pallets. They couldn't see anyone. They held their breath and listened. They couldn't hear anyone. They moved silently around the pallets to the other side of the building. A green, phone-booth-size, metal locker with vents in the door was bolted to the wall. Nicole moved down to the corner of the pallet stacks where she could watch the door to the warehouse. Ron picked the old dial lock on the locker. When he opened the locker door, Rickover, his wrists cuffed together with throwaway plastic cuffs, blinked back at him. His clothes smelled of sweat. His glasses leaned halfway down his nose, and his face was unshaven. Ron pulled him out of the locker. "Surprised to see us?"

"Not really. How long were you listening?"

"Long enough to know that you owe Philips money. He's a mob guy, isn't he? That's a big mistake."

"Tell me about it." Rickover held out his arms. "Have you got anything to cut this with?"

Ron ignored him. "Why aren't you dead?"

"Because the boss man wants to get paid."

Ron chuckled. "So you had us steal the Cellini to pay him back? I didn't think you had it in you."

"Yeah, well..."

Ron looked him up and down. "They turn out your pockets?"

Rickover pushed his glasses back up his nose with his cuffed hands. "What do you think?"

Nicole glanced down from the corner. "Let's get out of here."

"Cavity search?" Ron asked.

"They're not amateurs."

"So where is it hidden?"

Rickover shrugged.

"Come on, Ron," Nicole said. "You can do this when we're safe."

"Just a second." He looked at Rickover. "Kick off your shoes."

Rickover used one foot to push the shoe off the other foot. Ron picked up the left shoe, felt down to the end and pulled on the insole. It was glued in place. He dropped the shoe on the floor by Rickover's foot. He picked up the right shoe and went through the same process. This insole was loose. He pulled it out of the shoe. Taped to the bottom was a hotel keycard. "You did the same thing with the key to the hotel in Montreal. What's your room number?"

"Are you going to cut me loose?" Rickover asked.

"Room number?"

"Five o three."

Ron put the insole back in the shoe and dropped it at Rickover's feet. "Why did you set us up?"

"Set you up?"

"You nearly got us killed."

"The other guys weren't good enough to take the casket. I thought I was keeping you out of this trouble, okay? But you couldn't leave well enough alone, could you? If you hadn't got in a gunfight, the cops still wouldn't know the casket was missing."

"So you didn't send those guys to kill us?"

"Christ, Ron, how long have we known each other?"

"Ron," Nicole said, "we need to get out of here now."

"Okay, honey."

Rickover slipped on his shoes. Ron grabbed him by the shoulder. "Let's go."

"Why don't you just cut me loose? You can't walk me back to the hotel like this, so you might as well do it now."

"You're going to help us get the casket back. It's got to go to the museum."

"It's in the vault. Even you two can't break anything out of there. It would be easier to break someone out of death row. The Cellini casket is gone."

"You let us worry about coming and going. You just tell us what you know."

"Cut me loose first."

They walked back down the street toward the gate, and then turned into an alley headed north to get out of the sightline of the Crenshaw Industries warehouse. The buildings were smaller here. Dumpsters sat against the back walls of some buildings and construction debris was piled near the back walls of others. Nicole was walking point, her hand in her handbag, gripping her pistol. At an intersection, she saw something shift in her peripheral vision. She casually glanced in that direction. Was there someone behind the dumpster? After she got to the other side of the intersection, she waited for Ron and Rickover to catch up. "We might have a tail."

Ron frowned. "Where?"

"Tracking on my left."

Ron nonchalantly turned so that Nicole was blocking the view of him from her left as he shifted his gun from the back of his waistband to his right blazer pocket.

Nicole continued. "I'm going to backtrack."

"Okay," Ron said.

Ron and Rickover continued to the next intersection, Ron's left hand on Rickover's shoulder, Rickover still handcuffed, Ron's right hand on the gun in his pocket. "You know she's crazy," Rickover said. "No one's following us."

Ron smiled. "Like you would know."

They entered the next intersection. "Just so she doesn't shoot us accidentally," Rickover said.

"Stop."

They turned.

Rickover chuckled. "Hello, Grace."

A woman stood in the alley behind them. Her legs were spread in a firing stance, and she held her gun in both hands. Her dark hair lay loose on her shoulders. A shoulder bag hung at her side. "Get your hand out of your pocket."

Ron kept his hand on his gun. He could see Nicole watching them from the corner behind the woman.

"Your hand," the woman said.

Nicole stepped out from the corner with her gun pointed at the woman. "Set the gun down."

The woman glanced over her shoulder. Ron pulled his gun. She glanced from Nicole to Ron. She set her pistol on the ground.

Ron glanced at Rickover. "You know this woman?"

"Oh, yeah. Agent Grace Mosley, FBI."

Ron pushed him down the alley to Mosley, while Nicole came up behind her. Ron picked up her gun and pointed it at her head. Nicole put her gun away, frisked Mosley, and searched her shoulder bag. She pulled out an FBI ID and showed it to Ron. Ron pointed the gun at the ground. "Why are you following us?"

"You know why. I'm trailing a crew of art thieves."

"So are we."

"You're making me laugh. You passed the casket to Tommy Bartholomew, who gave it to Rickover."

"Then why are we here, dragging this idiot around? We need to get the casket back to the museum so you people will find something else to do, and we can go back to making a living."

"You expect me to believe that?"

"This kind of job attracts too much attention for us. You know the other players?"

"I followed them here. They led me to Rickover and then to you."

"If we're with them, why did we jailbreak this bozo?"

"Okay," Mosley said, "If you're really on the level, you bring me the casket."

"Now you're making *me* laugh. According to Aaron, the casket's in the freeport vault. All you have to do is go get it."

"By the time I can get a search warrant, it'll be gone. So you bring it to me without stirring up the NewTrust Corporation, and I'll forget about you."

Ron looked at Nicole. She shrugged.

He turned back at Mosley. "And you get the credit."

"Of course."

"And the case is closed."

"Absolutely."

"Okay, you've got a deal."

"What names are you using?"

Ron smiled. "Ron and Nicole Carter."

"If you get caught, I won't know you."

"Unless it gets you the casket."

"Of course. And I need Rickover. He's going to prison if he won't testify against his bosses."

"Whose locker is the casket in?" Ron asked.

Mosley looked at Rickover. "Tell him."

"Got a smartphone?" Rickover asked.

Mosley handed him her phone. He worked the phone with his handcuffed hands and Googled up a picture. "That's him. James Denison. He's staying in a suite at the Great Circle."

Rickover handed the phone to Ron. Nicole stepped over to look at the picture with him. James Denison had a confident smile. His gray hair and beard were clipped short. He was wearing a well-tailored blue suit. Ron glanced at Nicole to see if she was finished looking at the picture before he handed the phone back to Mosley. "How much did he pay you?" he asked.

"That's none of your business," Rickover said.

"That money is evidence," Mosley said, "so you can't have it. We done here?"

"How will we get in touch with you?"

"Don't worry. You get the casket, and I'll find you."

RON AND NICOLE were eating lunch at a table on the air-conditioned, glassed-in patio of the Tenderloin Shack. The place was noisy with conversation and the clacking of stoneware. The buffet line was busy with families. Servers dressed in jeans and golf shirts with the Tenderloin Shack logo on the pocket brought drinks to the tables and cleared away dishes so that the new customers coming off the buffet line would have a clean place to sit. Nicole pushed away a half-eaten plate of pork ribs, collard greens, and pinto beans and wiped her lips with her napkin. Ron reached across for one of her ribs. She pushed her plate a little closer to him and then got out her smartphone. She Googled James Denison. "Listen up," she said. "James Denison. He's fifty-seven. Trust fund baby. His grandfather developed some sort of coating for cardboard—go figure. He does hands-on charitable work: housing, counseling, job training for homeless women; mentoring program for aged-out foster kids. His wife is a sculptor. Naturalistic stuff. Two grown kids—a doctor and an art history professor." She looked up at Ron. "Hard to believe he's a bad player."

Ron washed down a mouthful of food with some iced tea. "Don't have to believe. He bought a stolen art object, so we know he's a bad player. Bad enough for us, anyway. And only God knows what he's got stashed in that freeport vault. Maybe we'll pick up a gratuity because of our good citizenship."

"You're always so optimistic. We've got to figure out our angle if we're going to get into that vault."

"You're right. And Aaron wasn't lying when he said we couldn't break in. We've got to get Denison to bring the casket out. Which means we need to spend a little time figuring him out. Why is he here? Was it just to pick up the casket, or has he got something else going on? We know he's staying at the Great Circle. Gambling, maybe? His wife into retro musicals? Are they into guided tours of the desert? We don't have time to become best buddies. We just need to figure him out enough to know where to apply the pressure." Ron wiped his hands with his napkin. "You ready?"

She leaned in close and whispered, "If we're going to track Denison, we're going to have to take our guns back to the hotel."

He grimaced. "I hate needing a gun and not having one. This job has too many moving parts. Rickover, Mosley, Philips's guys. None of them working for us. If this job was just about the money and not our freedom, I'd let it go."

RICKOVER AND MOSLEY were sitting on separate queen-size beds opposite each other in Mosley's hotel room on the seventh floor of the Great Circle Casino and Convention Center. Dirty room-service plates were scattered over the desk and bedside table. Rickover looked a wreck. His clothes were sweat-stained and dirty. He needed a shower and shave. He crowded his coffee cup onto the bedside table, pulled his legs up onto the bed, and leaned back against the headboard. Mosley sat watching him with a cup of coffee in her hand.

"You came along at the right time," Rickover said, "even though I would have liked to see you last night. Sleeping leaning up against the wall of a locker is a bitch."

"Took me longer to get here than I thought it would. My supervisor wanted to meet about the case."

"What did he want?"

"Homeland Security decided there was no terrorism involved and dumped the case on us, so he gave me the pep talk. It's early, so there's no real pressure yet."

"You'll be tying this up with a bow in a few more days."

"Hope so. The Carters—are they really trying to find the casket to return it?"

Rickover nodded. "Ron is a little different from your typical thief. Prefers to steal from people he thinks are crooks. As near as I can tell, they show up in a town, rip somebody off, and poof—they're gone."

"So how do you know them?"

"Sometimes, to avoid publicity and save money, the company would rather buy back an object from a thief than pay off the insured. The first time I met them was on a deal sort of like that. Other times, we've hired them to steal back objects that some other thieves stole."

"Company do that instead of reporting the theft to the police?"

"Yeah."

"Think they'll manage it this time?"

Rickover shook his head. "There is no way in hell. That vault is a death trap. The casket is perfectly safe where it is."

Mosley finished her coffee and stood up. "Well, at least your cover is holding up. Although I still think you're playing too close to the line. Philips's guys could have put a beating on you."

"They aren't going to really hurt me without Philips's okay, and Philips wants his money."

"I looked at the surveillance footage from the Charles Bay freeport. You didn't fake the theft, did you?"

"If the Cellini casket implicates Philips and get us into his vault locker, no one will care about how the bait was set."

"You sure about that? Did you tell Denison that the casket was stolen?'

"I didn't say it out loud, but he's no dummy. He negotiated to buy an important art object at a freeport on tribal land and made a cash down payment. He's got to know it was stolen."

"Even after I arrest Philips, it's still going to be tricky getting a search warrant here."

"I don't think so, but even if it is, we know where the casket is. The only way it could leave here is by plane or over the one bad road going north. So it's not getting away from us."

"And you're sure Philips's locker is full of evidence?"

"Why else would he go to so much trouble to hide it?"

She set her coffee cup on a room service tray. "I hope you're right. I've got to take care of some business. You look like death. Why don't you get cleaned up, take a nap? I'll be back later. Don't go out. Philips's guys are probably already looking for you."

RON AND NICOLE took up positions in the lobby of the Great Circle Hotel where they could watch the elevators, front desk, hallways to the casino, and the entertainment venues. Ron sat in a furniture grouping near the elevators with a newspaper and a paper cup of coffee, giving the appearance of a non-gambling hotel guest who was perhaps waiting for his wife to finish her spa treatment. Nicole sat across the lobby near the entrance to a bar, her smartphone in her hand, acting as if she were playing a game or writing a long text to someone back home. They sat most of the afternoon before they saw Denison come out of the elevators. Instead of a suit, he was wearing jeans, a black golf shirt, and a white linen sports coat, but it was definitely him. On his left hand was a wedding band, and on his right hand was a large topaz ring. He walked hurriedly out the main doors. Ron folded his newspaper and set it on the side table, dropped his coffee cup into a trash can, and followed.

Denison was on the sidewalk on the right side of the circle drive. Ron got out his phone, took a picture of the Indian on horseback sculpture, walked around on the right side of the drive, took another picture, and then joined the group of Chinese tourists out at the front of the drive for one last picture. In the meantime, Nicole had come out, slipped on a pair of movie-star sunglasses, put her phone to her ear as if she were taking a call, and started down the sidewalk after Denison. Denison was now about a half block ahead of her and a block ahead of Ron.

The day was hot and bright, and the low, brown mountains shimmered like an illusion in the distance. Faint noises from the airport and the waterpark carried on the breeze. Denison had his head down, as if he were on a city street somewhere with something important on his mind. Two Native American women in nurses' uniforms passed him on their way toward the business district. Without looking up, he turned up the sidewalk to the Nohamay Alternative Medicine Hospital, climbed the steps, and disappeared through the front door.

Nicole motioned with her hand as if she were hailing a cab, and then started after him. Ron ran to catch up. He was on the sidewalk coming up to the steps as she went through the front doors with her sunglasses in her hand. A moment later, Ron was standing beside her. "Where did he go?"

"I think he was in the left elevator, so he got off on the second floor."

Ron looked at the department listing. "Second floor is the Alternative Therapy Hospice Center. What's Denison's wife's name?"

Nicole Googled him on her smartphone. "Stacey Wert-Denison."

Ron went up to the information counter. "Could you give me Stacey Wert-Denison's room number?"

"Wert-Denison? Room two thirty-six."

Ron walked Nicole to the door. "He can't see you here. Go back to the hotel lobby and wait for him. I'll snoop around here."

Ron didn't want to end up in a face-to-face with Denison when the elevator doors opened, so he walked up to the second floor. He looked through the safety glass window in the fire door before walking out onto the second-floor lobby. Directly opposite the elevator was the nurses' station. Three women were busy inputting information onto screens. A sign indicated that room 236 was to the right. Ron moved steadily down the brightly painted hall, as if he knew exactly where he was going. When he came to room 236, he looked through the window in the door. Denison was sitting in a chair by the bed, but Ron couldn't see the person in the bed from his vantage point. He continued down the hall to the stairwell at the end and went back down to the first floor. He found an open chair in the lobby near the information counter, grabbed up an old copy of *Family Handyman* and sat down.

Two hours later, Denison came out of the elevator wiping his nose on his handkerchief. He went out the door with the same distracted look on his face that he had when he came in. Ron tossed down the magazine, took the elevator up to the second floor, and walked straight down to Stacey Wert-Denison's room. He pulled her chart from the wall rack by the door. He flipped through the pages. She had end-stage pancreatic cancer. She was on a treatment plan of herbs and medicines he'd never heard of, but it seemed as if nothing was helping. Ron slid the chart back into the rack and started for the stairwell at the end of the hall. He pulled out his phone.

"Nicki?"

"Yeah."

"He's on his way. The wife is dying of cancer. This is the last gasp, magical thinking attempt to save her."

"This is a tough play."

"Yeah, it's more girl next door than femme fatale."

"Okay. At least my outfit fits the part."

"It's just like every other play. We use what we know. He's depressed, already grieving; he's a hands-on, fix-the-world kind of guy. He's naturally looking for something to work on to ease his mind."

"I need to be his next project."

"Okay. What's your role?"

"Wronged woman. Floundering divorcee. Cheating husband left me. Don't know how to get control of my life. I'm drawn to casinos even though I'm a recovering gambling addict."

"You're the champ. He should be coming through the door any minute."

"Wish me luck."

Ron hurried out the front of the hospital, put on his sunglasses, and trotted down the front steps. He wanted to get back to the casino hotel in time to shadow Nicole when she made her play. Across the boulevard, engine noise broke the silence as an airplane rose up off the runway. Ron began jogging down the sidewalk. There were only a few people out—moms and dads with youngsters mainly. The adults without children were either in the casino or in their rooms, getting ready to go out for dinner. He slowed to a walk and caught his breath as he reached the circle drive to the casino hotel. He took off his sunglasses as he went through the lobby doors. Nicole was sitting in the same area as before, near the bar, her legs crossed, and her handbag in her lap. She touched her fingers to her lips, got up, and went down the hallway to the casino metal detectors. Ron looked around in the lobby for a few moments as if he were expecting to find someone, and then followed her.

Nicole drifted back through the casino. About half the slot machines were empty and there were only two customers at the first bar. The first three blackjack tables weren't even open yet, but Denison was standing at the fourth table. The blonde dealer, who seemed to be the bubbly, cheerleader type, wore a long-sleeved white blouse and fringed red vest. A pendant on a gold chain hung between her ample breasts. Nicole stepped up to Denison's right side just as he won the hand. "I see you've played this game before."

He turned and looked at her as if he were trying to place her, gave up and looked back at the dealer. The dealer looked at Nicole expectantly. She shook her head and held up her hands so that the surveillance cameras could see. Denison looked back at her. "You're not playing?"

"I'm barred from playing here."

He nodded to the dealer. She dealt him a card face down, and then dealt one to herself. He lifted the edge of his card. Seven of hearts. "Strange place to be if you can't play."

"You're right. I should know better. I just can't stay away."

The dealer dealt him a five of spades face up, and herself a ten of diamonds. He gave Nicole a searching glance before he turned back to his cards.

"Hit me."

The dealer dealt him a four of diamonds. "I'll stay."

The dealer nodded. She turned over a nine of clubs. "Nineteen."

Denison turned over his cards.

"Sixteen," the dealer said. She took his bet and his cards.

A redheaded waitress sidled up to his left side. "Drink, sir?"

Denison looked at Nicole. "You allowed to drink?"

She tilted her head and looked at him quizzically.

"Just trying to understand your parameters."

"Rum and Diet Coke, please."

"And I'll have a Jameson on the rocks."

The waitress disappeared. The dealer dealt. Denison looked at his card. "You here on vacation?"

"Just casting about, I guess."

"What do you do? You work here in the city?"

"I'm in between jobs, you know, trying to find my way, I guess. I've been living in Dallas."

"But you're not from there. Your accent—"

"No, I grew up in Iowa."

Their drinks came. "What about you?" she said.

"I mainly live in Palo Alto." He stuck out his hand. "I'm James Denison, by the way."

"Tracy Benet." She shook his hand. "Pleased to meet you."

"I probably seem a little nosey," he said. "Neither of us are kids. You seem to be starting over."

"That easy to tell, huh?"

Denison lost the hand and placed another bet.

"Hope I'm not distracting you from your game."

He shook his head. "I'm not really paying that much attention. Just trying to relax."

"I thought paying attention to the game was how you relaxed."

"Different for different people, I guess." The dealer gave him another card. He stayed. He won the hand and placed another bet.

He took a drink. He looked at Nicole very carefully. "You're not married."

She covered her left hand with her right. Her eyes teared up.

"I'm sorry. Guess that's a touchy subject." He took another card. "The only reason I ask is I was wondering if you would have dinner with me."

"What about your wife?"

"I don't want you to get the wrong impression. I'm only talking about dinner and some friendly chitchat in an expensive restaurant. I'm paying. I'm just looking for the company of someone who doesn't want anything from me. I thought maybe you were in a similar circumstance."

She smiled and nodded. "Well, when you put it that way." She drank from her drink. "Yes, I could use that kind of company."

He lost that hand and pocketed his remaining chips. As they walked out of the casino, she tipped her head toward Ron. She was beginning to feel the confidence that meant success.

RICKOVER WOKE UP, yawned, and glanced at the alarm-clock radio. Eight p.m. He'd fallen asleep at five. He got out of bed, but he wasn't ready to put on his dirty clothes, so he went to the closet and put on the hotel bathrobe that hung at one end of the row of Mosley's pants suits. Then he went into the bathroom and brushed his teeth with her toothbrush. He wondered where she was. Philips's men didn't know her, and she'd pulled the Carters into the game. What did she need to do that she couldn't do from here? Fortunately, he didn't need her to keep his plan moving. He picked up the hotel phone and chose an outside line. "Mr. Philips? It's Aaron. I've got your money."

"Where are you calling from? I'm not speaking to you anymore. Deal with my guys."

"I can't deal with your guys. They kidnapped me and tried to shake me down. I want to pay you and get your handshake that we're good."

Philips laughed. "And why should we be good? You tried to cheat me."

"Did I? That painting came out of a museum. We both know it. Why would I question the provenance of a painting hanging in a museum?" He walked over to the window and looked out on the desert. The moon sat just above the mountains, creating shadows along the near side. "The only thing I'm guilty of is trusting the judgment of the museum's experts. I gave the painting to you. You had it examined. How do you know your expert is smarter than the museum's? But did I bitch about it when you said you wanted your money back? No. I value our relationship."

"You've been dragging your feet."

"I've got your money now. I want to give it to you. I want the opportunity to do more work together."

"Stay put. I'll see what I can do."

Philips hung up. Rickover turned from the window and set the phone in its cradle. This was the hard part. The waiting. All the pieces of the puzzle were in place. Grace would arrest Philips when he was taking Denison's money. The chain of events would tie Philips to the casket in the vault at the freeport. It would be no stretch at all to get a warrant for Philips's locker based on a conspiracy charge. A federal judge wouldn't even blink. And the evidence in Philips's locker would send him to prison. Rickover smiled to himself. The number of cases that would be solved or pled out based on the contents of Philips's locker—this was a career-making, once-in-a-lifetime case.

Rickover looked at his wrinkled clothes lying out on the unused bed. He wasn't going to put them back on. When Grace came back, he'd call down to the front desk to replace the keycard Ron had taken and then send Grace to his room to get some clothes. He wanted to look rested and ready when Philips came to town.

NICOLE AND JAMES DENISON lay intertwined under the covers in the king-size bed in the bedroom of his hotel suite. Their clothes lay scattered in a trail that led from the living room sofa to the bed. They still had their underwear on. Nicole was taking it easy, letting him think that he was in charge, acting with the submissiveness of a woman used to abuse. She held his head in her hands as she kissed him, pressing her body against his, and felt his erection against her leg. He had his arms around her, holding her as tightly as the last piece of flotsam from the wreckage of his life as his lips and tongue and every breath moved in rhythm with hers. She reached down and felt the edge of the waistband of his boxer shorts. He jerked away from her and sat up on the edge of the bed, panting, hunched over, covering his erection with his hands. "I'm sorry. I'm so sorry. I can't do this," he said. "My wife has cancer. She's being treated at the hospital here. What we're doing—what I'm doing—is so wrong. I'm betraying her just when she needs me the most to be strong for her."

Nicole sat back on her heels behind him. The next few sentences were very important. "I know you're not the kind of guy who cheats and lies," she said slowly. "I know that's not you. How long have you been married?"

"Thirty-three years."

"I bet you two had some great times together. I bet most places you go, most of the things you do, remind you of her."

He started to cry.

She continued. "And now everything is broken, and it's all become too hard." She put her hand on his shoulder. "When you go to see her, does she know you're there?"

He shook his head.

She patted his back. "You're doing everything you can for her. You've got to keep yourself strong if you're going to continue to support her. You'll be no use to her if you fall apart. You have to do whatever you need to stay strong so you'll be ready to focus all your attention on her when she wakes up."

He turned his head toward her. "I can't."

"Shush," she whispered. "Lie down. Nothing is happening here. Lie down and let me hold you."

She pulled him gently back to the middle of the bed, kissed his forehead, and drew him down onto the bed. She wiped the tears from his face with the bed sheet. She put her arm around his shoulder, held his face against her breasts, and stroked his hair as if he were a small child.

"Relax," she said, "right now, in this minute, everything is okay. Leave the past in the past. Let tomorrow take care of tomorrow." She could feel the tension going out of him. "Shush." She smiled to herself. Denison didn't stand a chance. There was no player in him at all. And he was so sweet. And good-looking. Fucking him couldn't even be called work. But how was it that he was buying stolen art? That didn't fit his profile at all. "Shush," she said. His breathing became slow and even, but she kept whispering and stroking his hair.

"So you've been in touch with Philips?" Mosley was leaning against the desk in her hotel room with her arms crossed in front of her. Rickover, still in the hotel robe, was sitting on the unmade bed with his back against the headboard. A new room-service tray, stacked with fresh dirty dishes, sat on the unused bed.

"Yeah. I think I've got the hook in him."

"So when does he get here?"

"Don't know yet."

"So you still need to stay put."

"Speaking of which, can you go get me some clothes from my room?"

"If nobody's got it staked out, I'll bring them when I come back tomorrow."

"Tomorrow?"

"I've got to keep my cover up until we bust Philips."

"I thought we'd have some R and R while we were waiting for him to get here."

She sat on the edge of the bed beside him, put her hand on his thigh, and kissed him. "There'll be plenty of time to celebrate after the bust. You're single now, so we don't have to sneak around. It's just that right now I've got a few too many balls in the air. Bringing agents into Nohamay City without the city administrator finding out is a logistical nightmare. I need to be on my game if I'm going to have my people in place at the right time. So we catch Philips first, and then we party."

"It's just so boring here."

"I know it's a drag. Watch the pay-per-view if you like. I'll go get your new room key, and I'll bring your clothes in the morning."

Mosley left the hotel and walked the five blocks back to Clare's condo. The night sky seemed huge, much bigger than it did in the city. She shook her head to let the cool night breeze run through her hair. Aaron sounded as if he actually believed that Philips was going to fly into the city. His confidence was delusional. The best Aaron could hope for was not being blamed for the theft of the casket. His plan had never been very solid, and now it was about to blow back in his face, and he couldn't see it at all.

Sleeping with him had definitely been a mistake. It had been completely casual on her part—the word "love" had never slipped into their conversation—but he hadn't been able to hide their relationship from his wife. It was pretty amazing that he was as good of an investigator as he was when he was such a poor liar. And now he was running this entire investigation on his own so that he wouldn't have to share the credit, which meant he'd have no backup. He was entirely dependent on her help, and she couldn't help him when his chances of success were so poor.

Mosley unlocked the door to the condo, kicked off her shoes, and hung up her jacket in the closet. Clare would be off work in thirty minutes. Mosley went into the kitchenette and looked in the refrigerator. There was a package of pizza crusts in the freezer. She turned on the oven, got out a sauté pan, and sliced up some onion, mushroom, green pepper, and eggplant. She smeared some tomato sauce on a pizza crust while the vegetables cooked and added a teaspoon of garlic and some fresh basil to the pan as the peppers began to soften. Her phone rang. She took the pan off the heat and wiped her hands on the kitchen towel.

The incoming call was from Philips. "Yeah?"

"Got a call from your boy a little earlier."

"He told me."

"This foolishness has gone on long enough. You're going to turn him over to my guys."

"Why don't you just let me handle him? If you don't show, and your guy doesn't take the money, he's going to be boxed in. He can't go to the authorities without compromising himself—he stole the Cellini. Besides, the thieves he hired to steal the casket are snooping around. I've got them stealing it back from the buyer, so you won't go away empty-handed."

"You're not listening. Who do you work for?"

"I work for you."

"You're damn right you do. I shouldn't have to explain myself to you. You want your kid in a retard group home getting fucked over the lunch table by some high school dropout?"

"Mr. Philips, I..."

"I didn't think so. If you want her to stay at that country club for the developmentally disabled, you do what you're told. Where's he at?"

"I've got him in a room at the casino hotel."

"Room number?"

"703."

"I know you've been fooling around with him. You need some special time to say good-bye, you better get it done."

"Okay."

"And Grace, I like you. Please don't fuck with me. We both know how that will work out."

Mosley put her phone down on the kitchen counter. Her hands trembled. That conversation had gone completely wrong. Why had she thought Philips would respond to reason? All she had done was create doubts about herself. Aaron had misjudged the stakes he was playing for and now he was going to die. Mosley laid her hands on the edge of the counter and inhaled and exhaled as slowly as she could: one, two, three times. Fear was not her friend. Fear would wreck her plans.

She looked at the sautéed vegetables and the pizza crust. She needed to focus on that, regain her composure so that she could think clearly. She spooned the vegetables onto the crust, spread them out evenly, and sprinkled mozzarella cheese over them. She studied the finished pizza. That was better. She poured a glass of red wine from a bottle that was already open. She knew she was riding the tiger working for Philips. She'd always known she couldn't trust him, but she'd thought their relationship was special—that she was in a different category from his other employees. Now she knew just how wrong she was.

She sipped her wine. He could use her any way he saw fit, and there was nothing she could do about it. She'd already compromised herself by accepting his money. He could report her to the FBI, threaten Kelly, set his men on her. She had to find a way out. Being a courier was one thing; being an accessory to murder was unconscionable. When would he ask her to tamper with evidence? Or even commit murder herself?

The pizza. She'd forgotten all about it. She opened the oven and slid it inside. She shut the oven door, picked up her wine glass, and took a big gulp. Aaron had made his own bed. She'd tried to warn him. She couldn't think of any way she could still help him, but there had to be some way she could help herself. She couldn't go to her supervisor. She would lose her job, maybe land in jail. She was on her own. She needed leverage to use against Philips to guarantee her safety and keep the money flowing. Getting that leverage—that had to be her priority.

Clare came in the door wearing her blackjack dealer's uniform. "Hey, Grace." She slipped off her fringed red vest and tossed it onto the back of a chair and unzipped her black skirt and stepped out of it. "What smells so good?"

"I made a pizza. Thought you might like something to eat. It'll be ready in a few minutes."

Clare unbuttoned her white shirt as she walked toward the kitchenette. "What a night. My field of vision is full of playing-card after-images. Is there any wine open?"

Mosley poured her a glass and handed it to her over the counter-top. "There you are, sweets." Mosley felt empty and alone. She needed to keep Aaron out of her mind. He wasn't her responsibility, Kelly was. There had to be a way she could turn the tables on Philips. She tried to smile. She was so glad she would be snuggling with Clare tonight.

6

CRACKING THE VAULT

Ron and Nicole were eating a late breakfast at the same coffee shop they had eaten in yesterday. Their server, a young black woman with her hair in twists and a silver ring in her right nostril, had just refilled their coffee. Ron put his hands around his cup. "The toast here could be a little darker, and I don't know what's up with the aftertaste of the butter—I mean, it's still edible, but it's not quite right. The coffee, on the other hand, is perfect."

"You need to put some jelly on your toast," Nicole replied. She picked up a piece of bacon with her fingers, took a bite, and set it back down on her plate next to a half-eaten omelet.

Ron dabbed a corner of toast in the puddle of egg yolk on his plate and pushed it into his mouth. He washed it down with coffee and wiped his mouth with his napkin. "I won't need to eat again until supper."

He looked across the table at Nicole. "So let's go over last night one more time, just to be sure of the details. He couldn't close the deal?"

She smiled. "The equipment worked fine, but at the last minute guilt got the best of him. He cried; I helped him through his confession, held him like a baby until he fell asleep. Then I slipped out of there. Didn't think I'd be able to search the room without waking him up. Left a little note with my phone number."

"You're falling for him. I can tell."

"Look, I admit there's some heat, but I'm not falling for him. I feel sorry for him, okay? The love of his life is more or less dead, and he's taking it hard."

"Yeah, right. Are you sure he's not playing you?"

"There's no game in him. You should have seen him in the bedroom. He was like a virgin on his wedding night. He didn't even get me out of my underwear. If he told me he'd never slept with anyone other than his wife since they got married, I'd have believed him."

"But he does have feelings for you?"

"You saw the text he left me asking me to dinner tonight. He definitely wants me; that's why he's so guilty and confused."

"You are an absolute magician."

"Come on, Ronny, a regular guy just isn't a challenge. That's why I think we're wrong about him being a crook."

"He bought the jewelry box. Nobody made him. How much other stolen stuff has he bought over the years?"

"I'm just saying that we want to be careful."

"Of course we want to be careful. But don't let your emotions get the best of you. We've got to get the casket from Denison. It doesn't matter if he thinks it's stolen or not. We need to hand it over to Mosley and disappear. But that doesn't mean we can't be setting up something for the future if we play it right."

"I just want to get out of here. There's too much going on—the FBI and the mob crew—for us to get sidetracked."

"Well, Mosley's off our backs for now. Why don't you go back to the hotel and rest up for tonight. I'm going to try to find out where the mob guys are set up. We need to know more about them if we're going to stay out of their way."

. . .

James Denison sat in a chrome-framed chair pulled up to the side of his wife's bed at the Nohamay Alternative Medicine Hospital. A bank of medical machines, their sensors tethered to various places on her body, sat to the left of her bed. Two bags of liquid, one clear and one pale green, fed into the IV in her arm. He sat close enough to her to hold her boney, bruised hand while he watched her emaciated face for signs of consciousness. A red stocking cap covered her bald head. Her complexion had a yellowish tinge. Even though an oxygen tube was clipped to her nose, her breathing was ragged. Her eyelids fluttered, but her eyes didn't open. He spoke to her anyway.

"We're doing everything we can do. I know this is hard—harder than anything you've ever had to do—but the docs say there's still hope, so you've just got to hold on." He patted the back of her hand. "I talked to the kids this morning. Skip is angrier than Bell. He told me I was just being selfish bringing you here. That I needed to make my peace with the truth and let you go, just like he had. You know how he can get. He ambushed me with the 'I love you, Dad, but' thing like he was staging an intervention."

His eyes teared up. "It's hard seeing you like this, honey. I understand why it was too hard for the kids to go on. They can't imagine how you could possibly get better. But after you're well and back at home, they'll thank me for not giving up." The tears started down his face. "You're going to love the Cellini casket I got you. It's an amazing piece of work. I almost brought it with me just in case your eyes were open. But it's here at the locker, so you'll be able to see it first thing. I know you always wanted a Cellini. I wish I had got you one for your birthday last year. I don't know what I was thinking. But, anyway, I've got you one now. Just keep getting better."

Ron walked Nicole back to their hotel and watched her go inside to the elevators. The afternoon was heating up. His shirt was already wet where the Glock sat against his back under his sports coat, but he was happy to be carrying the gun. They hadn't seen any of Philips's crew since yesterday morning, and the only one they'd actually seen then had been outside the warehouse where they'd found Aaron, so Ron decided that was as good a place to start as any.

He moved quietly down the street between the warehouses. The only sounds were the laughing, yelling, and whooshing of water carried on the breeze from the Rising Rapids Waterpark across the boulevard. When he reached the Crenshaw Industries warehouse, he looked in through the window in the door. There was no one in sight. He picked the lock, cracked open the door and listened. Nothing. He slipped inside and walked around the pallets of boxes stacked in the middle of the room. The green metal locker stood open. He looked inside. It was clean: no personal effects, no scraps of paper, not even any dust. He examined the boxes on the pallets. They were supposed to contain computer monitors. He went back into the gap in the pallets where he and Nicole had hidden yesterday, pulled down a box, and opened it. Inside was a computer monitor. So this appeared to be a legitimate warehouse. Maybe it was part of a money-laundering scheme, but there was no obvious contraband here now. He closed the box and set it back in the stack with another box on top of it.

He left the warehouse, locking the door behind him, and walked down the street toward the airfield. Six airplane hangars stood in a row, their back ends facing the cluster of warehouses. Ron walked nonchalantly up the far side of the western-most hangar. To his right, a few hundred yards away, on the other side of a chain-link fence, was the public airport. He peeked around the front of the hangar. The overhead doors were closed. Looking down the row, he saw that only two hangars were open, with private jets parked in front of them. The nearer one had a Crenshaw Industries logo painted on its side. Two men, one white and one black, came down the steps from the private jet parked in front of that hangar, struggling with the weight of a long, heavy crate they were carrying between them. They lugged it into the hangar. Then the hangar's door rolled down.

Ron trotted back to the warehouses and turned down an alley to come up behind the Crenshaw Industries hangar. He slipped up along the side of the hangar until he reached the closest window and peered inside. The two men were opening the crate. Three other men, two black and one white, watched as they unpacked machine pistols, shotguns, and ammunition boxes onto a long table. The men were talking, but the noisy air conditioner hanging in a window at the back of the hangar drowned out their voices. Ron crept up to the next window in hopes of hearing what they were saying. The men were choosing weapons and opening ammunition boxes, but Ron still couldn't hear them clearly. The rumbling from the air conditioner was still too loud. He glanced down the side of the hangar; there was nowhere closer for him to listen.

He jogged back into the cluster of warehouses and made his way to the front gate and across the boulevard to the water park. Families were on the sidewalk, and he felt much safer mixed in with them. What were Philips's guys up to? They weren't here to rob the casino or the vault at the freeport. Those were fools' errands. Were they planning to reacquire Aaron? Did they think they were up against a rival crew? They had staked out the Charles Bay apartment when they were looking for Aaron, so Philips must have thought he and Nicole were connected with the casket, but it seemed like Philips's guys didn't know he and Nicole were here, and he needed to make sure it stayed that way. Time was running short. He fell in behind a family of four going back to their hotel in their swimsuits—mom in a beach cover-up, dad wearing a T-shirt, two boys with towels around their necks and flip-flops slapping the sidewalk. Ron got out his phone to call Nicole.

"Hey, honey. I found our friends. They came in on a private plane."

"So they're loaded up?"

"Yeah. And they look like they're going on a hunting party."

"What do you want to do?"

"Get our business done and stay out of their way."

"You sure?"

He slowed down and let the family get farther ahead of him. "I don't think they're looking for us. We're not that hard to find. I just wonder if they're willing to kill a Fed to take Aaron back."

. . .

NICOLE AND JAMES DENISON sat at a small table in the far corner of the dimly lit dining room of the Captain's Table Bistro, a small, dark wood and stained glass restaurant on the mezzanine floor of the casino hotel. The candle in the center of the white tablecloth cast a flickering light over their dinner dishes. "I thought I owed you an apology," Denison said. "I acted inappropriately last night." He rolled his eyes. "I'm sure I made quite a scene. I wanted to thank you for being so understanding."

"You don't have anything to apologize for. You're going through a difficult time. I looked up the hospital here online. This is your last resort, isn't it?"

"Mayo said there was nothing else to be done. But the docs here have an experimental treatment that helps about half the time, and they say Stacey is responding to treatment, so I'm still holding out hope."

"What else can you do? You can't give up."

"That's exactly what I think." He smiled a crumpled smile. "You're a very easy person to talk to. I just met you yesterday, and I feel like I've known you for years."

"Thanks for dinner."

"Do you have to go? Do you want to have a drink at the bar? Or would you like dessert?"

"I know what you're up to."

"What? No, I told you, yesterday was a mistake. I assure you, I—"

She cut in. "You don't want to be alone. When you're by yourself, you can't stop thinking about the worst. It's cycling through your mind, making you crazy. You're using me as a distraction."

He sighed and looked down at the tablecloth. "I must seem so obvious to you. Sometimes all of this is just a little overwhelming."

"So let's go to the bar."

When they got up, their server appeared. Denison handed him a credit card and told him to bring the bill into the bar. They went into the adjoining barroom. A few people sat at the dark oak bar near the

TV behind the counter, watching a boxing match. The sound was turned down. Soft jazz floated out of the sound system. Most of the booths were empty. They sat away from the TV. The bartender came over. He was a thin, narrow-faced man with steel gray hair. His white shirtsleeves were rolled up to his biceps. Denison looked at Nicole. "Drambuie, neat," she said.

"Make mine on the rocks," Denison said.

The bartender nodded and left.

Their server came in from the dining room with their bill, the credit card, and the credit card slip on a tray. Denison glanced at the bill, wrote in the tip on the credit card slip, and signed it. The bartender brought their drinks.

"Nature calls," Denison said. He got up and headed toward the restroom. Nicole reached her hand into her handbag, unscrewed the cap on a tiny bottle, looked over to see that the bartender was busy with another customer, slid Denison's highball glass into the middle of the table, and poured a clear liquid into his glass. Then she pushed his glass back to where it had been. A few minutes later he was back in his seat.

"Yesterday, when I asked if you were on vacation, you said you were drifting."

"Guess I should share a little honesty. Two months ago I got divorced. I was blindsided. Didn't know it was coming."

"That must have been hard."

"I have a gambling problem. My ex started running around on me while I was at the casino." She sipped her drink.

"So now you're drifting, which means?"

"I have to figure out what do with myself. I know this sounds crazy, but I'd like to have what you and your wife have. I want someone to love me so much that they can't let go, no matter what happens."

He reached across the table and patted her hand.

She continued. "But I don't want to bore you with my little problems. You've got enough on your plate."

He sipped his drink. "Nobody's problems are small to them. I can't help you with the love interest, but I might be able to help you with other parts of your drift problem. Are you going to need a job at some point? What kind of work skills do you have?"

"I appreciate your thoughtfulness, but how about if we talk about something else? I could get depressed in my room."

"Okay, okay, I understand. But if you want my help, just say the word."

"Thanks."

She finished her drink. "Do you want another?" he asked.

She shook her head. "I should turn in."

"I'll walk with you." He drained his drink. They got up. She waited while he paid at the bar, and then they walked out into the mezzanine lobby to go to the elevator. He stumbled and steadied himself against the wall.

"You okay?" she asked.

"Yeah," he said, "I was having such a good time; I guess I didn't realize how much I had to drink."

She slipped her arm through his. "Let me help you."

As they waited for the elevator, she could feel more of his weight shift onto her. The door opened. A couple wearing casual summer clothes got out. They gave Denison a questioning look. The man said, "Do you need help, ma'am?"

"No, thanks," Nicole said. "We're fine."

"This is embarrassing," Denison said.

Nicole helped Denison onto the elevator and leaned him up in the corner. His eyes were half-closed. She texted Ron with an exclamation point, and then she reached into Denison's jacket pocket for his room keycard, swiped it through the reader, and pressed the button for the top floor. He looked like he was asleep on his feet. The elevator opened at the fourth floor. Ron got on. They continued to the top floor. Ron put Denison's arm over his shoulder and grabbed him around the waist. "James," he said sharply, "time to walk."

Denison stumbled out of the elevator, Ron half-carrying him. Nicole went on ahead of them and opened the door to Denison's suite. Ron walked Denison through the living room into the bedroom and unloaded him onto the bed. After Ron pushed him onto his back, put a pillow under his head, and took off his shoes, he pushed three fingers into Denison's neck to check his pulse and then peeled open one of his eyes.

"How is he?" Nicole asked.

"He's hammered. Pulse and breathing are fine."

"Great." She kissed Denison's forehead. "Sweet dreams."

Ron glanced around the bedroom. "Why don't you start in here?"

Nicole started going through the dresser drawers. There was underwear in one, socks in another. The rest were empty. In the closet there were three sports coats with empty pockets, four pairs of pants, ditto, and six golf shirts. A suitcase in the floor contained an assortment of women's clothes. She went into the bathroom. Shaving kit in the top drawer of the granite-topped sink—nothing unusual there—other drawers empty. She went out to the living room. Ron was going through the drawers under the maple TV cabinet. "You finding anything?"

"Nothing in the desk."

She pulled up the cushions on the sofa. It was a hide-a-bed, but nothing was hidden there. She opened the mini-fridge. Nothing but the usual assortment of overpriced beverages and snacks. She pictured Denison coming into the room with a briefcase or a folder or some papers in his hands. He's beat. He plops down on the sofa. Sets whatever is in his hand on the cushion or on the end table. Gets up. Gets something to drink. Sits back down. Goes over the papers. No, not his style. Picks up the remote control. So where did the papers go? She turned to Ron. "Give me a hand with the sofa."

They dragged the sofa out from the wall. Under the side by the end table, a large white envelope lay on the carpet. She picked it up. The return address read "Nohamay Mountain Vault." She smiled at Ron. "Bingo."

They sat down on the sofa without pushing it back to the wall. Ron pulled the papers out of the envelope. "Okay," he said, running his finger down the first page, "they keep casino hours, so it's twenty-four seven." He turned to the second page. "And here's the locker number, and here's the twelve-digit access code." He went to the third page. "We also need a—they call it a medallion—to get through security." He shook out the envelope.

Nicole went back into the bedroom. Denison was sleeping peacefully. She put her hand in his right front pocket. Coins, key ring, and a restaurant receipt, but no medallion. She slid the objects back into the pocket. She emptied his left front pocket. Smartphone. She put it back. She lifted his wallet from the inside pocket of his linen jacket. In one of the credit card slots was a card from the vault with a gold medallion printed on the front. She kept the card and put the wallet back.

Ron was standing in the doorway behind her. "Find anything?"

"I think I've got it."

Nicole came back into the living room. They pushed the sofa back to the wall and checked the rooms to make sure everything was back in place before they sat back down. Ron read through the paperwork again. "This is a new account. It's in both their names. But she went straight from the airplane to the hospital bed, so smart money says they've never seen her."

"They might have a picture of her."

"Sure. And there might be some code we don't know about. It's a crapshoot. Wouldn't try it if there weren't so much at stake. You up for this?"

She nodded. "It'll work. Walk in and walk out. No risk of hijackers this time."

Nicole put the locker number and access code into her smartphone. They left his room keycard on the end table and slid the vault envelope back under the end of the sofa. Next, they stopped off at their hotel room. Nicole changed into loose khaki pants, a black scooped-neck top, and a khaki jacket. She fixed her make-up to make her face look hospital pale and covered her hair with a scarf. Ron got his Glock and his Smith & Wesson from the room safe. Once out of their hotel, they walked up a deserted side street. A tan minivan, a red Lexus and a black Jeep Cherokee were parked along the street. Ron broke into the Cherokee, and they drove it past the water park and the private airfield to the parking lot in front of the Nohamay Mountain Vault. Security cameras were mounted on the light poles. Four cars were parked at the far end of the lot. Ron pulled up to the front doors. He took Nicole's hand in his. "You look exactly the part. Don't walk too fast."

"I've got this. Piece of cake."

"What's your name?"

"Stacey Wert-Denison."

"Why are you coming here in the middle of the night?"

"Not that it's any of your business, but my skin can't take the sun. Cancer treatment." She kissed him. "Enough of this."

She got out of the Jeep and walked up the well-lit steps as if she weren't used to walking, gripping the steel rail and taking each step deliberately. When she got to the top, a heavyset security guard—a white man with a shaved head—opened the thick glass door. "Thank you," she said.

She walked to the security counter. Another guard, this one a lanky Native American with a military haircut, asked for her medallion and swiped it through a reader. "Mrs. Wert-Denison?"

"Yes."

"Step through the metal detector."

She put her handbag on the counter and stepped through the metal detector. The guard looked in her bag and handed it back to her. "Step over to the fingerprint scanner, ma'am."

"What's this all about?"

"Just our usual overnight procedure, ma'am." He raised the cover on a flat scanner that sat next to a computer on the counter. "Place your right hand here, please."

She laid her hand palm down on the scanner. Were Stacey Wert-Denison's fingerprints in the database? The scan of Nicole's hand came up on the computer screen. "Looks good," the guard said.

"Great. Can I go to my locker now?"

"Just waiting for verification."

Just as the verification came back as a mismatch, Nicole spun on her heels and ran. The guard looked up from his screen. "Hey!" He pressed the alarm button. A siren wailed.

For Nicole, it was as if she were running in quicksand. The bolts in the heavy front door slid home. The shaved-head guard charged toward her like a football lineman rushing the quarterback. She looked over her shoulder. The Native American guard was only a few steps away, his gun in his hand. There was nowhere to run. She sat down on the floor with her back to the glass front wall, brought her knees up to her chest, and wrapped her arms around them.

HALFWAY ACROSS THE PARKING LOT, Ron sat with his hands on the steering wheel, the Jeep in Drive, his foot on the brake, watching the front doors to the vault. He knew Nicole could sell it—that wasn't an issue—but if it all went south there was only one door, and that's where the armed guards were. He heard the alarm sound. He unlocked the passenger door so that she would be able to jump in when he pulled up to the bottom of the steps. He held his breath, his eyes locked on the heavy glass doors, willing the doors open. He could see shapes inside, but he couldn't make out what was going on. Come on, Nicki—push through the door. The alarms stopped. The doors didn't swing open. Nicole didn't come running down the steps, the Cellini casket in her arms. Ron turned off the Jeep. They'd missed their chance at the casket. Now it was all damage control: follow them when they brought Nicole out of the vault, kill whoever he had to, spring Nicole, and then go on the run. He patted the Glock under his jacket. He had to stay focused. There was no more room for error.

MOSLEY AND RICKOVER were sitting on separate beds in Mosley's hotel room, Rickover wearing the clean jeans and shirt that she'd brought for him. Both of the beds were made, and there was only one room-service tray of dirty dishes on the desk in the corner. "I'm sorry I haven't been able to be here more," Mosley said, "but I've got nearly all of the arrangements in place. If Philips comes now, he doesn't stand a chance."

"When he comes."

"Have you heard back from him?"

"Not yet. I'm not surprised. He's very careful. Tomorrow or the next day I'm betting he'll call."

There was a knock on the door. Mosley opened it. A tall black man, wearing khakis and a black nylon jacket, stood in the doorway. "I'm Gary. Mr. Philips sent me."

Mosley stepped out of the way. Gary came in, followed by two similarly dressed white men guiding a hotel luggage cart. On the cart rode an empty, extra-large, dark green duffel bag. Rickover sprang up from the bed. "You? How did you find me?"

Gary and the nearer white man, a bodybuilder with a blond crew cut, grabbed Rickover by his arms. Rickover turned to Mosley. "You're a cop, for Christ's sake. Do something."

Gary chuckled. "You should see the look on your face."

Mosley's stomach churned. She avoided Rickover's eyes. "I tried to warn you off, Aaron, tried to protect you, but you wouldn't listen."

Rickover turned to Gary. "You can't do this. I made a deal with your boss."

"That's right," he said, "and this is the deal."

They let go of his arms. Before he could move, the other white man, smaller and potbellied, Tased him. He dropped to the floor. Gary laid out the duffel on the carpet next to Rickover. The two men lifted Rickover by his arms and legs and set him into the duffel, where they taped his mouth and handcuffed his wrists and ankles with plastic handcuffs. Then they folded him up, zipped the duffel closed, and heaved it onto the luggage cart.

Gary turned to Mosley. "You got the money or the object?"

"I'm working on it."

"You better work harder. Mr. Philips wants the money or the object. Preferably both."

Gary held the door open, and his men guided the cart into the hall. "You know how the boss is. Do your job."

The door shut. Mosley sat on the end of the bed with her head in her hands. Just what kind of person was she? There must have been some other way, but she hadn't even tried to think of it. She had just handed Aaron over.

Her mouth was so dry she couldn't swallow. She got up, got a bottle of water off the metal tray on the desk, and opened it. The truth was that she wasn't willing to sacrifice her career to save Aaron's life. That was the bottom line. If she lost her job or went to prison, Kelly would be the one to suffer. She drank the water. It felt good going down her throat. And why should she sacrifice herself for Aaron? Because she was an FBI agent? He cheated Philips. He dragged her into his plan without consulting her. He stole the Cellini casket.

She'd told him he was in over his head, but he wouldn't listen to reason. It was the same egotism that cost him his marriage, and he hadn't learned a thing. Tears started down her cheeks. She set the water bottle down, pulled some tissues from the box on the desk, and blew her nose. He was exactly the kind of idiot who got himself killed. She went into the bathroom and splashed cold water on her face. She had to find a way out—something that would guarantee her freedom and pay for Kelly's school. She needed the kind of evidence that Aaron had failed to get. She dried her face with a towel. She had to stop thinking about Aaron. There was nothing more she could do. She glanced at her watch. Clare would be off work soon. She went down to the casino to find her.

7

RETURNING THE CASKET

Nicole sat in a straight-backed chair in the middle of a windowless storeroom inside the Nohamay Mountain Vault, her head hanging as if she were asleep. A bare bulb hung from the ceiling above her. The two security guards and the night manager had brought her here, gently but firmly, and cuffed her ankles and wrists to the chair with plastic handcuffs before they left. Her handbag sat on a nearby table. Boxes of bathroom supplies were stacked on the shelves along one wall. A security camera covered the room from the corner above the door. Nicole figured it must be morning by now. Her back ached and her feet tingled from inactivity. No one had come to move her out of the vault. That was a bad sign. They were keeping her capture a secret. The fewer people who knew, the easier it would be to kill her. And if they chose to kill her here, Ron would never have the opportunity to rescue her.

She took a deep breath. She had to hold onto hope. She'd given herself up to the job when she'd walked through the metal detectors. No one had shown up to interrogate her yet. Would she be able to manipulate that person? Could she make him feel sorry for her? She needed to seem as vulnerable as possible. Even more helpless than she really was. She peed in her pants. A big wet stain grew in her lap and down her right leg, urine dripping into a puddle beside her shoe. Then she bit her lip until she tasted blood. There. She'd made herself seem as pathetic as she could. The trick now was not to panic, not to think about being tortured, not to think about the last time she was tortured, but to instead be ready to take advantage of any new opportunity, to work those advantages until Ron could make his move.

R<small>ON</small> <small>YAWNED</small> and glanced at his watch: 7:25 a.m. Nicole was still inside the vault. Why? Four cars in the parking lot. Four to six nightshift employees. Management, security, maybe custodial. When was the shift change? Were they being held late? When did the daytime employees arrive? Eight thirty? The bosses couldn't possibly want them to find out about the attempted break-in. It was the worst possible publicity. So management would squash any potential gossip. The overnight employees could be bought off. A nice bonus and a pat on the back. But they had to get Nicole out of the vault. Killing her was a step too far for the hourly help. Sweat trickled under his arms. He'd need a SWAT team to force his way in. A black SUV pulled up to the front door. James Denison and a short, thin Asian man climbed out and started up the steps. Ron smiled to himself. Finally, an opportunity.

T<small>HE</small> <small>DOOR</small> to the storeroom opened. Nicole lifted her head slowly. James Denison, his face pasty and his eyes bloodshot, came into the room accompanied by an Asian man who had a grey buzz cut and wore a black suit with a white shirt and silver tie. Denison rubbed his bearded chin. "I had to see it to believe it. You really did try to masquerade as Stacey to break into my locker."

"Hello, James."

"My God, what's that smell? You've wet yourself."

"It's been a long night."

The Asian man spoke with an American accent. "Ms. Benet. I'm

Bobby Lee, the general manager of Nohamay Mountain Vault. You already know Mr. Denison."

She nodded.

"I've been briefing Mr. Denison about you and your associate, Anthony Rose, apologizing for letting the two of you stay in the city after you were picked up at the casino."

"We told the casino manager we wouldn't gamble."

"No, instead you tried to rob Mr. Denison's locker."

"Turn me over to the tribal police."

"By our agreement with the Nohamay Nation, the tribal police have no jurisdiction here, Ms. Benet. Malefactors leave on a plane or end up in a grave. And right now, that depends on your cooperation."

Nicole looked at Denison. "You look worse for wear. I'm sorry I drugged you. How do you feel?"

"You're amazing," Denison replied. "You've already been caught. You're tied to a chair, facing God knows what, and you still sound so sincere. Why did you do this? Did you choose me in particular or was I a random target?"

"Do you want me to tell you in front of Mr. Lee?"

"I've got nothing to hide. I'm not afraid of your lies. Go ahead."

"Okay," Nicole said. "The Cellini casket that you put a down payment on a few days ago is stolen property."

"That's absurd."

"You paid cash, right?"

Denison didn't say anything.

"The casket was stolen from a freeport in Charles Bay while it was in transit to the Peter Damascus Sculpture Museum in Los Angeles. It has to be returned. There's an undercover FBI agent here who I'm retrieving it for."

"That casket wasn't stolen."

"The guy you bought it from—bald, gray, wire-rim glasses. I don't know what he told you, but his real name is Aaron Rickover. He's an insurance investigator with Metropolitan Assurance. That's how he got the information to steal the casket. Why do you think it was so cheap?"

"You're going to tell the truth or I'm going to leave you with these guys."

"You say there's an FBI agent here?" Lee said.

"She's here."

"The FBI is supposed to notify us before they come to the city."

Nicole shrugged. "I don't know anything about that."

"What's her name?"

"Grace Mosley."

Lee took out his smartphone and began tapping the screen with both thumbs. He looked up from the screen. "Grace Mosley is an FBI agent who specializes in art theft. Excuse me a moment. I have to call the city manager." He put his phone to his ear and turned to the wall.

"This is unbelievable," Denison said. "Just because there's a FBI agent named Grace Mosley doesn't mean you're working for her and the casket was stolen."

Lee put his phone away and turned back to them. "Ms. Benet, Mr. Rose is here asking for you."

The door to the storeroom opened. The lanky Native American security guard pushed Ron into the room. "Mr. Rose," Lee said, "I'm surprised you came here of your own volition."

Ron spoke to Nicole. "Are you okay, Tracy?"

"Tony," Nicole said, "I've told them the truth—that we're helping Agent Mosley."

Denison looked from one to the other. "All you've given us is a story. Where's the proof?"

"Go online," Ron said. "Go to the *Charles Bay Gazette* for two days ago and four days ago. The stories are right there. Late Sunday evening the casket was stolen. On Tuesday a man was murdered at a parking garage. Go ahead. Check it out."

Denison took out his phone. "I don't have a signal in here."

"We have a secure net in the vault," Lee said. "I'll use my phone." He looked up the *Charles Bay Gazette*. "Here's the first article." He handed his phone to Denison.

Denison read the articles and handed the phone back to Lee.

"This is so hard to believe. I was just trying to do something nice for my wife."

"It's not your fault," Nicole said. "You've been distracted because of your wife's health issues. That's what made you an easy target."

Ron turned to Lee. "How about cutting her loose?"

Lee nodded to the security guard, who cut the plastic handcuffs at Nicole's wrists and ankles. She stood up slowly, rubbing her wrists.

"Why didn't you just tell me the truth to begin with?" Denison asked.

"Would you have believed me? Besides, we didn't know if you were Rickover's accomplice or not."

Denison's eyes lit up. "Oh, no. If this gets out in the media, my reputation will be shot. My kids, the foundation…" He turned to Mr. Lee. "You've got to find this Rickover guy."

"One step at a time, Mr. Denison. We need to be absolutely certain that these two are telling the truth before we move forward. The newspaper describes a theft, but it doesn't give very many details about the object. Let's contact Agent Mosley and verify the information. If she is in the city, we'll go together with the casket to meet her. We'll be able to see her credentials and confirm that she is the same person as the one in the FBI database. If it all checks out, we'll put out an alert for Aaron Rickover."

"I need a change of clothes," Nicole said.

Lee nodded. "I'm sure something can be arranged."

RON, Nicole, Denison, Lee and two security guards rode over to the casino hotel in a city SUV with tinted windows. The whir of the air conditioner fan was the only noise inside. They parked in a loading dock at the side of the building and entered the hotel lobby from the hallway to the elevators, the blue-suited security guards carrying the crate inside a large, black duffel bag. Mosley sat in the lobby on a sofa with her back to the wall, a red wheeled suitcase on the carpet next to her. She was dressed in her FBI uniform: black pantsuit, white shirt, hair pulled back at the nape of her neck. Mr. Lee led the way.

Mosley stood up when they reached her. The two of them shook hands.

"Sit down, everyone," Mosley said. She took out her ID and passed it to Lee.

He read it, nodded, and handed it back. "We have the casket."

"Thank you for your cooperation." She opened the red suitcase. "Could you have your men put it in here?"

Lee nodded toward the security guards. They took the crate out of the black duffel and placed it into the roller case. It was a snug fit.

"Sure that case is strong enough?" one of the guards asked.

"It'll be fine," she replied.

"Agent Mosley," Denison said, "Why didn't you just come to me when you knew I had the casket?"

"What if you denied you had it? You might do that even if you weren't Rickover's partner. There wasn't enough evidence to get a warrant, not here—not with NewTrust fighting me every step of the way. And once you knew I was after the casket, I didn't want to play cat and mouse. I'm sorry, Mr. Denison, but I couldn't take that chance."

"Where's Rickover now?" Ron asked.

"And where's my money?" Denison asked.

"Rickover's already on a flight back to Charles Bay, where federal agents are waiting at the gate. I'm sure he'll give up the money as part of the plea bargain, and then we'll give it back." She took a business card out of her handbag. "Here's my card with my personal phone number. We'll need to interview you about how the casket came into your possession, but that can wait."

"When does the casket go to the museum?" Nicole asked.

"We'll be in contact with Peter Damascus tomorrow at the latest. Then it's just a matter of making arrangements."

"So we're done?" Ron said.

Mosley nodded. "As far as I'm concerned."

"Agent Mosley," Lee said, "the FBI is supposed to contact us before they come to the city."

"Of course. But this was exigent circumstance. When I came here,

I was one step behind the casket. We didn't know then that Mr. Denison had it, and we couldn't take the chance that Rickover and the casket would disappear while we made the usual arrangements."

"Just the same, our city manager, Mr. Chen, will be filing a protest."

"I understand. Anything else?"

"How much longer do you plan to be here?"

"I'll be leaving tomorrow."

Lee grunted and nodded. Everyone stood up, except for Mosley. Denison turned to Nicole. "I guess I owe you an apology. You're one of the good guys. What I don't understand is why once you knew I was innocent, you didn't just tell me the truth."

"I'm sorry about all that, James, but Agent Mosley couldn't just take my word, so we had to go forward with our plan. It's all lame, I know, but that's how we ended up here."

"So the time we spent together, me unburdening myself, the connection I felt with you, that was all—"

"That was all real, James. The facts weren't real. I'm not divorced. I'm not a gambling addict. But the emotions were real. My empathy is real. I really do hope your wife gets better. I really do feel sorry about this horrible situation that you're going through."

"I hope you mean that. It's hard to know what you actually feel when you always sound so believable."

Lee and the security guards started walking back toward the loading dock. Denison, Nicole, and Ron headed toward the front doors. Denison and Nicole were still talking. Ron drifted further back as they moved along. Mosley watched them all walk away. She didn't want to make small talk, invent vague plans, or account for her whereabouts. After they had all been gone for a few minutes, she stood up and rolled the red suitcase toward the elevators.

Once she was in her room, she'd call Philips, and he could make arrangements to collect the casket. Then all she had to do was make a reasonable attempt to find Aaron's money and she could go home.

She'd tell her superiors she followed the casket here, but never found it. As she was waiting for the elevator, it occurred to her that the only people who knew she had the casket were people who couldn't betray her without exposing themselves. The Carters didn't want any law enforcement to know they were connected with the robbery. Denison didn't want his reputation muddied by the press finding out he'd been involved. And Lee didn't want anyone to find out that there had been an attempted break-in at the vault or that the vault had been sheltering stolen property.

The elevator doors opened. She wheeled the suitcase in. The door shut. Philips didn't yet know she had the casket. She swiped her room keycard and pressed the seventh-floor button. The elevator rose.

She had three choices. One, she could return the casket to the museum, which was what she should do. It was stolen property. She had a sworn duty to return it to its rightful owner. But if she did, Philips would know that she'd betrayed him. He'd exert even more pressure on her; ask her to commit even worse crimes to prove her loyalty. And if she refused, he would threaten to expose her criminality, and she and Kelly would suffer.

Two, she could just follow the plan and give the casket to Philips and stay in his good graces. But she'd still be under his thumb. And he'd have another criminal act to blackmail her with. He was demanding and paranoid. He'd already pushed her from courier to accessory to kidnapping. There was no way of knowing what he might want her to do next.

Or, three, she could just keep the casket, lay low for a while, and then sell it. The money would pay for a lot of semesters at Clear Skies. Philips wouldn't know she'd collected it if she didn't return it to the museum. And there was no way the FBI could prove she had the casket without the testimony of the Carters, Denison, or Lee.

Could she manage to hold onto it? Could she sell it without getting caught? Aaron was probably dead. But Philips's men wouldn't dare kill her; she was an FBI agent. The weight of the world would come down on them if they tried. And if Aaron were dead, maybe there was a way she could connect Philips with his murder. She had a hard link between Aaron and three of Philips's men—they'd taken him from her room. Philips had told her he was sending them, but that was just her word against his. If only she'd made a recording. She needed a hard link between one of those guys and Philips. Or a confession. It might be doable. If Aaron were dead. Then she'd have as much on Philips as he had on her. She'd be completely free.

She felt dizzy. She leaned her head against the elevator wall. God, what was she thinking? Had she really fallen so low? She should be hoping that Aaron was alive. She had delivered him to Philips's men. If he were dead, it was as much her fault as theirs. The three choices flitted back and forth in her mind. The elevator doors opened at her floor. She couldn't decide what to do. She pressed the lobby button. All she knew for certain was that she wasn't going to stash the casket in her room, and she wasn't going to tell Philips that she had it. The door closed. She had to take it somewhere else for safekeeping.

DENISON AND NICOLE sat at a glass-topped table on the deck of the Sunburst Lounge with their drinks and their empty dessert plates. A jazz quartet situated just inside the restaurant was interpreting soul ballads, the trumpet player adding in some occasional scat singing. The sun had dropped behind the shrub-covered mountains, making the clouds glow red behind, and a cool breeze was beginning to flow down to the lowlands. The servers were moving among the tables, turning on the gas space heaters. Denison leaned on the table. "So why did Chen call you Tracy Benet?"

Nicole smiled. "We ended up in the 'no gambling' database on a different job. Casino management spotted us on their cameras."

"So you were using aliases?"

"Yes."

"And you work for the FBI?"

She shook her head. "It's complicated." She drank from her margarita.

He looked at her quizzically.

"Let me put it this way: we rob crooks."

"Is that the truth?"

"What have you seen us do? You aren't a crook, of course, but the casket was stolen. So we were going to steal it back."

He pushed the tray with his signed credit card slip on it out of the way. "How do you tell if someone's a crook?"

"Believe me, that's usually the easy part."

"And that's how you make a living?"

"Yeah, that's what we do." She sipped her drink.

"So why did you agree to come to dinner with me? Why aren't you off somewhere with Ron? Your job is done."

"I wasn't lying when I said I really felt for you. The way you care about your wife—you're an admirable man, James. I just want to help if I can."

His phone rang. He looked at the screen. "I'm sorry. I need to take this." He put the phone to his ear. "Yes?"

Nicole watched his eyelids flutter.

"Thanks. I'm coming right over." He put his phone away. "Stacey has taken a turn for the worse. I'm going over to see her."

They both stood up. "I'll go with you," Nicole said.

"You don't have to."

"I want to. You shouldn't be by yourself."

Denison and Nicole zigzagged through the tables on their way to the interior of the restaurant and the elevator lobby beyond. He seemed lost in thought, and Nicole didn't interrupt him. When they were out in front of the hotel, on the sidewalk walking toward the hospital, he finally spoke. "Are you sure you're up for this?"

"I'm okay."

"She's been sick a long time. Emaciated as if she's anorexic. My son wants to have me declared temporarily incompetent if I won't let her go."

"It's hard to know what the right thing to do is."

"Yeah, it really is. I don't blame him. I understand his feelings. He thinks I'm losing it."

Outside of the hospital, Denison stopped on the front steps and took a deep breath. Then they went up to Stacey's room. Stacey lay with her eyes closed, her breathing like a grating hinge, the machines near her head making their satisfied noises. He pulled the chair around next to her bed, sat down, and took her boney hand. It felt colder than it ought to. Nicole stood behind him with her hands on his shoulders. He sat for a few moments looking at Stacey, and then he reached forward and ran his hand down the side of her ruined face. "You've never seen what she used to look like, have you?"

"No," Nicole said.

"God, she was so beautiful. And everything she touched she made beautiful." His voice cracked. He got out his handkerchief and blew his nose. "We did a lot of good things in this world together. She was the one who got me started on mentoring the foster kids. I got all the credit, but it was really because of her." He put his handkerchief in his lap. "But that didn't get her any dispensation. Two years of increasing misery. And to end up like this."

Nicole patted his shoulders. "You can't make sense out of this. It's just not possible. There's nothing logical about it."

"Don't," he said. "Don't say anything. I still don't know if I can trust you."

8
PLAN B

In the early morning before the sun rose above the mountains, a couple walking their dog on the outskirts of the city found a body wrapped in a rug that appeared to have been dug up by a coyote. The body was taken to the emergency department at the hospital. Fred Chen, the city manager, received a phone call from his security chief, Doug Wounded-Bear, while he was still getting dressed.

"Pick up the FBI agent, Rose and Benet, and Mr. Denison. Bring them to my office," he said in his slightly Asian accent. "Be very polite, but don't accept no for an answer." He knotted his paisley necktie, sipped his coffee, and looked at himself in the mirror. Charcoal pinstripe suit, white shirt, and wingtip shoes. He looked like a man to be reckoned with. He put on a silver and turquoise bracelet. He was going to make this problem disappear before lunch.

He was sitting behind his antique oak desk when Wounded-Bear, a large man with chiseled features who could have been a retired wrestling coach, escorted Mosley, Denison, Ron, and Nicole into his office. Chen didn't offer anyone a seat. "You've heard the news?"

They all nodded. He looked at Mosley. "So you put Mr. Rickover on a plane?"

Mosley frowned. "This is terrible. I've known Rickover for years. I thought I'd talked some sense into him. How was he killed?"

"We're not sure of the cause of death just yet."

"One of his accomplices must have caught up with him before he got to the airport. That's the only scenario that makes sense."

"So now you're telling me there are killers in my city. You created this trouble by not doing your job. You should have taken him to the airport."

"My job was to recover the casket, not babysit Rickover."

"You're bad for business. I want you gone, and I want your assurances that you won't tell your superiors about this matter."

"How can I avoid that?"

"You don't tell about the murder, and we don't tell about you sanctioning the break-in of our vault. Do we understand each other?"

She nodded.

He pointed at Nicole and Ron. "And you two have worn out your welcome as well. You'll tell no one about this unfortunate incident, and you'll never come back here. If you come back, you won't leave, understand?"

"Loud and clear," Ron said.

"And, finally, Mr. Denison, I know you were innocent in all this, but we expect your cooperation as well. If the break-in or the murder become public knowledge, your reputation will be hurt as much as ours."

"You expect me to help you cover up a murder?"

"We are the legitimate authorities here, Mr. Denison. Just because we wish to proceed quietly doesn't mean we won't capture and punish the killer."

"When you put it like that."

"So we can count on your discretion?"

He nodded.

"Excellent. Enjoy your stay in Nohamay City."

Wounded-Bear escorted them out of the city offices building. The sprinkler system was watering a row of bushes newly planted along the sidewalk.

"Take a deep breath," Wounded-Bear said, looking directly at Ron and Nicole. "Freshly shoveled dirt is the last thing you'll smell if you don't get out of town."

They watched the glass door close behind him.

Ron turned to the others. "Hard to believe Aaron is dead. Even if my first thought was to kill him for roping us into this mess. He had two kids and an ex who were counting on him." He looked at Mosley. "We handed him to you, and you lost him. What kind of clusterfuck was that?"

"Hey, you weren't his only friend. He was supposed to get on the plane, salvage his career."

"Who do you think killed him? Did he have any partners?"

She shrugged. "I don't have the slightest idea. But I'm going to find out. I'm going to make sure his family gets closure."

"You still have the casket?" Ron asked.

"For now."

"When does it go to the museum?"

Mosley looked from Ron and Nicole to Denison and back again. Was this an opportunity to get paid for the casket without having to stash it for a year or more? None of these three could expose her without exposing themselves. "That's an open question. Maybe it never goes."

"What does that mean? It has to go," Nicole said.

Denison cut in. "I thought we had this straightened out. It goes to the museum, and no one finds out I was involved."

Mosley continued. "You heard Chen. They're going to cover up Aaron's murder. With him out of the picture, the evidence trail is dead. The casket could have disappeared with him. Airline records show he came here, but after that there's not going to be any information. So if either of you want it returned, I've got to be paid. Two hundred thousand, and the casket goes to the museum."

"We don't have two hundred thousand," Ron said.

"You'd rather have the FBI hunting you for the theft than find a way to scrape up the cash?"

"The museum will give you a one-hundred-and-fifty-thousand-dollars finder's fee," Nicole said.

Mosley laughed. "Even if that were true, it wouldn't apply to law enforcement." She turned to Denison. "How about you? How badly do you want the casket to go back to the museum?"

"Why should I pay?"

"Think it through. It's just a one-time payment. Something to compensate me for the trouble you've caused."

"The trouble I've caused?"

"Buying stolen property. Interfering in a police investigation. Might have got to Aaron in time if he hadn't sold the casket to you."

"I'm already out one hundred thousand."

"Not my problem."

"How do I know you'll keep your word this time?"

"Don't be so cynical. Just get the money ready. I'll be in touch." Mosley left them standing in front of the city offices.

Denison turned to Ron and Nicole. "How can she do this?"

Ron shrugged sympathetically. "You tried to buy the stolen casket, so you can't go to the cops. You could claim it was a mistake, probably get off, but the case would still make all the scandal websites. You're in the gray world now, where leeches like her can tax you whenever they want."

"Did you two have anything to do with this?"

"We got suckered into this mess back in Charles Bay," Ron said. "If the casket doesn't go to the museum, and Mosley doesn't shield us, eventually the cops are going to be coming after us."

"James," Nicole said, "our anonymity is our most important asset. We can't work if people know who we are."

"Do you think she's right? That I have to pay her?"

"No. Maybe. Depends on how you play it," Ron said. "She can't afford to be exposed, either, so we've got a little elbow room. If the casket goes to the museum, you're in the clear, just like us. So we need to find out where she's hiding it and take it."

Ron turned to Nicole. "How many guys are we up against? I saw five at the Crenshaw Industries airplane hangar. Anybody else?"

"That was all of them."

Denison interrupted. "Crenshaw Industries?"

"There's a crew of thugs operating out of the Crenshaw Industries warehouse," Ron said. "We've been trying to stay out of their way."

"What do they look like?"

Nicole said, "We've seen three black guys and two white guys, all dressed like they're modeling for a sporting goods catalogue."

Ron continued. "So maybe five to seven guys were after Aaron. We know Mosley bends the rules, but we don't know how far. Is she with them or is she on her own? Somebody killed that guy back in Charles Bay. And somebody killed Aaron. Was it the same somebody, or just a coincidence?"

"What are you saying?" Denison asked. "Are you saying those guys killed Rickover over the casket? Are we in danger here?"

"Of course we're in danger. I'm just trying to figure out how much," Ron said.

Denison's mouth fell open. "What if they think I still have the casket? I've got to call the hospital." He took out his phone. "Hello? This is James Denison. Has anyone been to see my wife?" He listened for a few seconds. "Thanks." He put his phone back in his pants pocket. "She's safe."

"For now," Ron said. "Do you have any juice with the management here?"

"What do you mean?"

"Will they provide a security detail for your wife?"

"I could ask."

"Why don't you go back in, talk to Chen, see if they'll provide security. Don't tell him about Mosley's threat or the Crenshaw crew. We want to keep the Mosley thing between ourselves."

"Why? Why don't we want all of them arrested?"

"James," Nicole said, "we're the only people who need the casket returned, so we're the only people we can trust. Everyone else has their own agenda. And maybe you want to call in your own security people. Once your team is in place, then you know you and your wife are safe."

"Okay," Denison said.

"And one more thing," Ron said. "See if they'll let you look at their on-street security camera footage. We might get lucky and find out if Mosley is working alone or if she's part of that Crenshaw crew."

Denison nodded. "What are you two going to do?"

"We're going to try to find the casket," Ron said.

DENISON WENT BACK into the reception area of the city offices building. A large Native American rug featuring a red and white zigzag pattern on a gray background hung from the right wall. The windows in the left wall looked out over the front lawn of the city offices. Wounded-Bear was gone. A small, thin woman sat behind the desk, furiously keyboarding on a laptop. "Excuse me," Denison said, "I'd like to see Mr. Chen."

The woman finished inputting her thought before she looked up at him. "Do you have an appointment?"

"No."

"Wait a minute." She wagged her finger thoughtfully. "You're—"

"James Denison."

"Right." She picked up her phone. "Mr. Chen? Mr. Denison is here." She smiled. "Go on in."

Chen closed his laptop when Denison came into his office. "Please sit down," he said. "What can I do for you?"

"Mr. Chen, I have some concerns I'd like to talk to you about."

Chen nodded.

"This is how it appears to me. I got the casket from Rickover. Rickover's been killed. I gave the casket to Mosley, so I can't give it to the killers if they come for me or my wife. My wife's in the hospital and can't be moved, so I want a security detail for her."

Chen shook his head. "I'm sorry, Mr. Denison."

"Just until my security team can get here. Twenty-four hours at the most."

"I understand why you would be worried, Mr. Denison. And we do want your business. But if we provide special security for your wife, there will be no way to contain the information. It will become a status symbol. All the high rollers will want special security. Besides, it's unnecessary. Everyone is safe in Nohamay City."

"Like Rickover?"

"That was an unfortunate, isolated incident, which he brought with him."

"Which is still ongoing. Are you investigating?"

"Our security personnel have the situation well in hand."

"What makes you think you'll find the killers before someone else gets hurt?"

"Relax, Mr. Denison. There is nowhere to hide in Nohamay City. If the assailants are still here, we will find them."

WHEN RON and Nicole got back to their hotel room, Ron opened the room safe and laid the guns out on the nearest bed. "Where do you think we stand with Denison?"

Nicole picked up one of the Glocks, ejected the clip and checked the breach out of habit, and then reinserted the clip. "I think he's with us, for now, but he'll only cooperate if he thinks we're helping him and his wife."

"She's already gone."

"But he's not ready to believe it." She put the Glock in her handbag.

Ron checked the other Glock and put it in the holster at the small of his back. "We've got two problems. We need to figure out what the Crenshaw guys are up to. They must have killed Aaron, but why did Philips send them here?"

Nicole nodded. "They're our only suspects; that's for sure."

"If they're after the casket, then Mosley probably isn't in with them, unless she's planning to double-cross Philips, and she seems to be smarter than that. We have to get out ahead of these guys before this job blows up. We need to get our hands on the casket. Pronto. So if we can't steal it from Mosley, we need to convince Denison to buy it."

"I'd rather steal it," Nicole said.

"Absolutely. We don't need Denison in the picture, making things more complicated; we just might not have a choice. That's why you need to keep spinning him."

Nicole's phone rang. She looked at the screen. "It's Denison."

"Answer it."

"Hey, James, what's up?"

She looked at Ron. "The city won't help."

"Won't help? I'll fix that. Tell him to go to his hotel room and wait for Chen's call. His wife will be safe. I'll be watching her."

She relayed the message and put her phone away. "He sounded skeptical."

"Good. He'll be all the more impressed when I pull it off."

"What are you going to do?"

"Create an incident." He laid his Glock in its holster back on the bed and got down on one knee to strap on the .38's ankle holster. "And then I'm going to use the keycard we took off Rickover to have a look in his hotel room."

"Need any help?"

"Tell you what. Leave the gun here and start following Mosley. See if anyone is watching her. Maybe you'll find out where she's hiding the casket. You know she's not keeping it in her room."

RON DUCKED into a knickknack shop on the corner next to the water park and elbowed his way through the families pawing over the merchandise. By the checkout was a locked case of silver and turquoise jewelry. Racks of swimsuits and T-shirts filled the center aisles. On the walls were displays of minerals, fake arrowheads, Native American ceramics made in China, toy guns, toy bows and arrows, puzzles, and cowboy and Indian costumes in children's and adults' sizes. He searched through the facemasks—Indian princess, warrior, blonde-wig cowgirl, Lone Ranger—before he settled on a rubber facemask depicting a banged-up cowboy with a black eye and his tongue hanging out. The gum-chewing, teenage Native American girl behind the checkout counter looked at the mask and then at him. "Let me guess. Costume bachelor's party."

"You got me," he said.

"Never changes." She handed him his receipt. "Have a nice day."

Out on the sidewalk, he rolled the mask up and put it in his blazer pocket. It was late enough in the morning now for the sidewalks to be busy with vacationers going to brunch or to the water park or to the casino for some early gambling. He walked past the front of the casino-hotel and down to the hospital, where he went around to the side entrance and up the stairs at the end of the hall. In the second-floor stairwell, he looked through the safety glass window in the door. The hallway was empty. He cracked the door and listened. All quiet. He moved silently down the hall to Stacey Wert-Denison's room. Denison had done as he was told. Stacey was by herself.

Ron stepped into the bathroom in her room and put on the cowboy mask, taking care to tuck it into the collar of his jacket. Then he locked the room door open and went to her bed, unlocked the wheels, and unplugged the wires from the monitors, tossing the wires over her body. Moving quickly, he pushed her bed out into the hall just as the alarms from the disconnected equipment started going off at the nurses' station.

A nurse, a heavyset woman with a blonde ponytail, started down the hall, shrieked when she saw him, and yelled back over her shoulder. A thin Native American woman and a huge Native American man with a buzz cut came running. Ron wobbled the bed sideways so that it blocked the hall and ran back the way he had come. He bounded down the steps in the stairwell two at a time, pulled off his mask on the first-floor landing, pushed through the door to the first floor, shrugged out of his jacket as he fast-walked down the hall, and then rolled the jacket up and shoved it under his arm. He ducked into the men's restroom near the information counter in the lobby, put the mask in the trash, and ran his hand through his hair. Then he came back out into the hall and sauntered up to the information counter just as the huge nurse with the buzz cut pulled open the stairwell door and came barreling toward him. "Excuse me," Ron said to the receptionist behind the counter, "Bill Jenkins isn't in his room."

A dark-haired woman with freckles on her face looked up from her computer screen. "Just a second. I'll check for you." She tapped some keys on her keyboard. "He's at physical therapy. Are you family?"

"No, just a friend."

"Visitors' hours are noon to eight."

Just then the huge nurse put his hand on Ron's shoulder. "Hey you, what are you doing here?"

Ron looked up into his face. "I'm here to visit a friend, but I guess I have to come back later."

"Really? You just got here?"

"What's this about?"

The nurse studied Ron's eyes. "I don't believe you. What you got rolled up under your arm?"

"Get your hand off me," Ron said.

"Let me see what you got." He reached for Ron's jacket with his free hand. Ron knocked the nurse's hand off his shoulder and stepped back. He turned to the receptionist. "Could you call your supervisor, please?"

The nurse pointed his finger at Ron. "There's something not right about you."

"I don't know what's going on around here, but I'm leaving," Ron said. He turned on his heels and pushed through the door. As he walked down the steps in front of the hospital, he called Nicole on his phone. "Hey, honey, you can tell Denison to expect a call from Chen."

"That was quick. How did it go?"

"No problem at all. You find Mosley?"

"No luck yet."

"I'm on my way to Rickover's hotel room." He put his phone back in his pocket as he walked down the sidewalk to the boulevard.

UP ON THE SECOND FLOOR, the two nurses moved Wert-Denison back into her room and reconnected the monitors. While the thin nurse checked Wert-Denison over, the heavyset nurse went back to the nursing station to call Dr. O'Brian, the hospital administrator, but when she got there, Dr. O'Brian was already hurrying off the elevator. O'Brian was a slightly built Native American woman dressed in khaki slacks, a blue open-collared shirt and a white doctor's coat. Her gray-streaked hair was tucked behind her ears. "What's going on up here?"

"A crazy guy in a Halloween mask tried to take away Mrs. Wert-Denison."

"Is she okay?"

The ponytailed nurse nodded. "Larry chased after the guy. He hasn't come back yet."

"Larry Smithfield?"

"Yeah."

O'Brian got out her cell phone as she strode down the hall to Wert-Denison's room. "Mr. Chen? You told me to keep you informed of any unusual situations."

"Yes?"

"Somebody tried to take Mrs. Wert-Denison out of the hospital."

"You can't be serious." The line was quiet for a moment. "Who?"

"We don't know. He was wearing a mask. One of our people chased after him."

"Keep someone with her until a security officer gets there."

"Yes, sir."

"And have the staff write down exactly what they saw while it's still fresh in their minds. Mr. Wounded-Bear will send an investigator."

CHEN HUNG UP HIS PHONE. He looked out his window down to the street. Today appeared to be as peaceful and ordinary as any other day. It needed to stay that way. He should warn Bobby Lee and Jason Stands-Alone to be on the alert. But first things first. He speed-dialed Wounded-Bear and explained what had happened. "Send an investigator and a female security officer to the hospital."

"Yes, sir. Right away."

"Any leads in the Rickover investigation?"

"We're just getting started. We're trying to find his hotel room, but it's not listed under his name."

"We've had two incidents in twenty-four hours. This must not continue."

"Yes, sir."

He ended the phone call, but he was still holding the phone in his hand. There was no good reason to put this off. He called Denison's hotel suite. "Mr. Denison? It's Mr. Chen."

"What can I do for you?"

"There's been an incident at the hospital involving your wife."

"My wife? Is she okay?"

"She's fine."

"What happened?"

"It appears that someone tried to take her away."

"Someone tried to kidnap her? I warned you. I told you she needed protection."

"Mr. Denison, she's fine. She hasn't been harmed. There's a security officer on the way to her room as we speak."

"I'm going over there."

"Mr. Denison, I'm very sorry I didn't take your concerns more seriously. We've never had an incident like this before. Did you call your own people?"

"Yeah. They'll be here tomorrow."

"They will have our full cooperation. Mr. Denison, I'm sorry about all of this. Is there anything else I can do for you?"

"Can I look at the security camera footage from the streets to see if anyone was following Rickover?"

"Just in case his killer might be after your wife? Our cameras aren't set up to facilitate such a search, Mr. Denison, but if you want to view the video footage, we'd be happy to accommodate you."

RON USED the keycard to open the door to Rickover's hotel room. It was a standard room with one queen-size bed. The curtains were partially open, and the bed was made. A few shirts and pants hung in the closet. He went through the pockets. They were empty. He glanced in the bathroom, but he didn't see a shaving kit. One of the drawers in the cabinet under the TV contained socks and underwear. He went back to the closet, pulled out the suitcase, and opened it. Nothing. He got down on his hands and knees in front of the room safe. Just another device designed to keep the cleaning staff honest.

He had it open in a few minutes. Inside the safe he found a file folder. He took it to the table by the window and sat down to go through it. On top was a two-page summary outlining Rickover's scheme to implicate Philips in the theft of the Cellini casket, with the intent of getting access to his freeport locker at the Nohamay Mountain Vault. Poor bastard. Hard to believe he really thought such a simple plan would fool a gangster like Philips.

Ron looked at the next document. It was a gym membership agreement for the hotel fitness center and spa. With it was a gym pass, which had what appeared to be a locker number and locker combination written on it. Rickover didn't play sports—not that Ron knew of—and he definitely didn't work out. Ron stood up and looked carefully around the room. He'd checked everywhere, but just in case, he lifted the edges of the mattress and felt underneath. Nothing.

Ron took the elevator down to the mezzanine level. A young woman wearing designer yoga wear, her brown hair pulled up on top of her head, stood behind the counter at the entry to the spa. He showed her the gym pass. She input the member number into her computer and gave him a nod. He pushed through the door into the empty men's locker room, found the locker, and entered the combination. On the shelves in the locker were a towel, gym clothes, cross trainers, and a gym bag. He unzipped the gym bag. Inside were several banded bundles of one hundred dollar bills. Jackpot.

He stuck his hand into the bag and flipped through the bundles. Ten, which meant $100,000. Had to be Denison's money. Part of the physical evidence of the casket changing hands. What was up with Rickover? How could he be sure the money wouldn't disappear from the locker? Why had he been so confident he could take down Philips? Where was his backup? Had Mosley been in on it with him? And if so, why had she folded? Or had she really thought he'd gotten on the plane and was out of harm's way? He zipped up the gym bag and pulled it out of the locker. The money was his now. He nodded to the receptionist on his way out of the spa.

Denison sat in his wife's room, holding her boney hand. Nothing had changed. She was exactly the same as she had been yesterday and the day before that and the day before that: yellow skin; sunken eyes; shallow, raspy breath. The herbs and supplements weren't helping at all. Even he had to finally admit it. Maybe it had been a mistake to bring her here. Maybe the kids had been right. But he just couldn't give up if there were even the slightest chance. How could he live without her? What was he going to do? He sighed, and laid her hand down. As he got up to leave, Dr. O'Brian rapped on the door and entered the room.

"Mr. Denison. I heard you were here. I just wanted to say how sorry we are about the incident."

"Stacey looks the same."

"We examined her. Being moved into the hallway didn't affect her."

"And her prognosis?"

"Would you like to sit down out at the nurses' station?"

He shook his head.

"When you first contacted us, and we looked at her records, we felt we had a thirty percent chance of being able to help her. Unfortunately, sometimes medical science isn't strong enough to overcome a particular illness."

He started to tremble. "So you're saying that she..."

Dr. O'Brian put her hand on his arm. "I'm so sorry."

"How much time?"

"I don't know. No one can know. Soon."

He glanced back at his wife, and then he looked past Dr. O'Brian to the open door. His eyes were wet with tears.

"Are you sure you wouldn't like to sit down?" she asked.

"No, I've got somewhere I need to go."

He walked past the female security guard sitting in a chair by the door to Stacey's room without really looking at her. He needed to stop thinking. He needed something to do so that he could stop thinking about the decisions he'd made. He raised his arm and blotted his tears with his sleeve. He'd really known that Stacey was going to die for some time; he just hadn't been ready to accept it. Dr. O'Brian had merely confirmed what he really knew in his heart. It didn't change anything. He could still protect Stacey and make sure that she was comfortable.

Someone had tried to kidnap her—maybe someone who was part of that Crenshaw gang. Or was that Ron? Was it all just a ploy to get Stacey a security detail? He didn't know. He needed something to do. There was nothing more he could do at the hospital, but there was still the surveillance footage to look at. Maybe he could find out if Mosley was working with the Crenshaw gang. He could do that. That was something he could do—something that could occupy his mind so he wouldn't have to think about the choices he'd made and the choices he'd have to make.

RON SQUINTED against the light reflected off the pavement as he came out of the side door from the lobby of the Great Circle Casino Hotel with the gym bag in his hand. It was time to set up plan B. They needed to be ready to run if they couldn't get the casket, and now they had the money to make it happen. He turned left up a side street and walked toward the old part of town where the permanent residents lived. In a potholed gas station parking lot, he saw an old Camry with faded red paint and a cracked right front bumper. There was a For Sale sign on the windshield. Maybe he was on a lucky streak. He went into the gas station. The glass front door was smudged with greasy fingerprints and a thick layer of dust covered the counters. The window air conditioner rumbled softly. A teenaged Native American wearing a black tank top with a picture of Jimi Hendrix on the front sat on a stool behind the counter, and a white man with bad skin and a gray ponytail and mustache, his red check flannel shirt rolled up his forearms, sat in a folding chair up against the far wall.

"How much for the car?" Ron asked.

The teenager looked at the old man. The old man sat back in his chair and rubbed his chin. "Haven't really given it much thought. What's it worth to you?"

"Does it run?"

He nodded.

"You have a clear title?"

"Uh-huh."

"Five thousand."

The old man chuckled. "I don't guess you've ever bought a car around these parts before. I'd take twenty for it."

"How old is it?"

"It's nine years old."

"Nine years old? I'd be Santa Claus giving you ten thousand. Bet you haven't done any maintenance on it."

The old man stood up and spat on his hand. "Ten thousand it is."

"Eight thousand."

He shook his head. "Ten thousand."

"I'm bringing it back if it doesn't run right."

The old man shrugged. "Mister, you won't ever see me again."

Ron shook the old man's hand. They went out to the Camry. The old man got out the keys, sat down in the driver's seat with the door open, and started the engine. It roared to life on the first turn of the key. Ron looked inside. The upholstery was badly faded from the sun on the passengers' side, as if the car had always been parked in the same place, and there were cigarette burns on the seat. The old man glanced at him. Ron nodded. The old man got out, took the car title out of his billfold, unfolded it onto the hood of the car, and signed it over to Ron. Ron took the title and compared the VIN to the metal plate on the Camry. "Let me see your driver's license."

Ron compared the name on the license with the name on the title. "Looks good." Ron reached into the gym bag and pulled out a bundle of one hundred dollar bills.

The old man smiled broadly, revealing a set of brown-stained teeth. "Thank you kindly."

"You bet."

The old man walked back into the gas station. Ron got out his phone. "Nicole? I've got some good news."

"Really?"

He told her about finding Rickover's $100,000 and then tripping over their getaway vehicle.

"That's great. We deserve a few breaks. You going to put a starter disconnect on the car?" she asked.

"Don't you think that's overkill?"

"It would be crazy if we were running to the car with Philips's guys behind us and the car was gone."

"Our luck has been pretty bad lately, hasn't it? I'll see what I can do."

Ron walked back into the gas station. "Is there an auto parts store in town?"

The old man nodded. "Yep. Taber's, over on Sundog Road. West end of town. They can do about anything."

NICOLE STOOD in the casino by a pillar between one of the bars and the blackjack tables. Grace Mosley was at an otherwise empty blackjack table, sitting on a stool and talking with the dealer, a full-figured blonde in a knee-length black skirt, a white shirt unbuttoned to show her cleavage, and a red, black-fringed vest. They weren't touching, and they definitely weren't flirting, but something about their interaction seemed intimate.

When Mosley got up to leave, Nicole thought she saw—what was it? Something about the dealer's eyes, the way she laid her hand on the edge of the table, the way she exhaled. Nicole's eyes flitted back and forth between Mosley and the dealer as Mosley walked away. The dealer watched Mosley until she was out of sight, but Mosley never turned to look back. Could it be? Could the blackjack dealer be in love with Mosley? And what was Mosley doing about it? She'd slept with Rickover—maybe even helped him wreck his marriage. Was she sleeping with this woman as well?

Nicole trailed after Mosley, staying well behind her so she wouldn't be noticed, but when Mosley started down the hallway to the hotel, Nicole stopped and turned around. Something was going on with the blackjack dealer—something that wasn't casino business. Maybe she and Mosley were lovers. Maybe they were just friends. Maybe they were just both connected to Philips or the Crenshaw crew. Whatever it was, it seemed that the dealer might be in a part of Mosley's life that she and Ron didn't know anything about, and that part of Mosley's life, if it existed, would provide an excellent place for her to hide the casket.

Nicole took a seat at the bar where she had a good view of the blackjack tables, ordered a glass of merlot, and asked for a menu. She'd have some late lunch and chat up the bartender. She needed to know when the casino work shifts changed and where the employees' entrance was located if she were going to follow the dealer home.

RON FOUND Taber's Auto Parts between a QuickGas and a McDonalds in the last strip mall at the west edge of town. A long time ago, he'd been taught a trick for disabling a car. It was probably not necessary, but Nicole was right, the way this deal had been going, a little paranoia was probably in order. The parking lot was empty. A bell rang when Ron went through the front door. An unshaven man with a ragged mustache, wearing blue coveralls with the name Jay Taber embroidered on the pocket, stood behind the counter. "Can I help you?"

"I need a remote car starter with the starter disconnect."

"Really? We don't have much call for them around here. Folks mainly need them in cold weather."

"But do you have one in stock and can you install it?"

"Let me check my inventory." He shifted to a grease-smudged desktop computer on the counter and keyed in the information. "No remote car starter."

Ron started to turn away.

"Hold on, buddy." Taber clicked through several pages before he looked up. "Okay, I think I've got you hooked up. I've got a car alarm system that includes a remote car starter. Last year's model. It'll cost you a little more than the remote car starter."

"But does it have the starter disconnect?"

He squinted at the specifications. "Yeah, sure does."

"Can you install it for me?"

He peered out the front windows. "What you driving?"

"A 2007 Camry."

"I can get you fixed up, no problem. Pull around into the bay in the back."

Ron sat on a folding chair nursing a Coke while Taber installed and tested the car alarm system. Then he drove back toward the hotel, circling around until he found a supervised parking deck that appeared to be mostly full. He waved at the uniformed attendant as he drove in. On the second level he found a spot in full view of the security cameras. He popped the trunk and looked inside. There was a rusty white metal box labeled First Aid, fast-food wrappers and used to-go cups, a couple of wadded-up oil-stained blankets, and a car jack and tire iron, but no spare tire. He pushed the gym bag containing the $90,000 down into the wheel well where the spare should have been and set the wheel well cover back in place before he adjusted the junk to make it look as if no one had opened the wheel well. He slammed the trunk lid, locked the car, set the car alarm and starter disconnect with the remote, and walked toward the stairwell.

Then he stopped, turned around, and looked at the car. Perfectly camouflaged. No one was going to bother that beater. It wasn't worth the trouble. Every other car on the deck was more valuable. Now he and Nicole were no longer dependent on the airport, and if anyone did try to steal the car, they'd have a hell of a time trying to figure out why it wouldn't start. He continued to the stairwell and came out on a side street one block over from their hotel. As he walked toward the hotel entrance, he noticed two of the Crenshaw crew—the guy with the blond crew cut and the black guy with the goatee—moving toward him.

NICOLE WAS STANDING by a parking deck on the shaded side of the street across from the employees' entrance to the casino. The blonde blackjack dealer—Clare, according to the bartender—no longer wearing her fringed vest, walked out onto the sidewalk talking with a redheaded man dressed in a cook's white jacket. They walked to the corner together, and then Clare crossed the street and walked north into a residential area of small houses with dusty, grassless yards. Trash cans were out at the curb as if it were trash day. In some yards, small children played on swing sets or dug in the sand with beach tools. In others, wash hung out on clotheslines to dry. Nicole followed the dealer three blocks to a row of stucco one-story condos with tile-red doors. Clare went into condo number 893 D. Nicole walked by the front of the condo and continued down to the end of the row. Then she got out her phone and called Ron. His phone rang—eight, nine, ten rings—and then turned over to voice mail.

"Ron," she said, "I've got a lead, I think. Call me as soon as you can."

DENISON SAT at a computer monitor in the security office of the city offices building. Wounded-Bear sat beside him, going over some paperwork spread out on the desk in front of him and occasionally looking over at the on-street security camera footage that Denison was viewing. Denison had already looked at the footage from the last two days at three important intersections and found nothing. Now he was looking at the footage of the main intersection between the casino and the airport. This footage, like the others, was grainy and most people appeared indistinct as they moved through the intersection with the walk light, because the system was only designed to give an overall view of the intersections to aid in traffic control and accident response.

Denison stopped the film for a better look whenever he thought he'd found something. He'd seen Mosley, or a person he thought was Mosley, and he'd seen some men dressed in business casual wear who might have been in the Crenshaw crew, but he hadn't seen them together, and he hadn't seen Rickover even once. He rubbed his eyes. Thus far, this exercise had been a complete waste of time. All that was left was today's footage. Rickover wouldn't be on it, but he had nothing better to do.

He saw four figures who he knew were Mosley and Ron and Nicole and himself. Then he saw two men dressed business casual, one black and one white, taking someone through the intersection in the direction of the airport. He squinted. Was it Ron? He shifted his eyes to see if Wounded-Bear were watching and then closed the computer program.

"Find anything?" Wounded-Bear asked, without looking up from the report he was marking up with a pencil.

"No."

"Can't say I'm surprised. Anything else I can do for you?"

Denison shook his head. "I'm going back to my hotel."

Wounded-Bear looked up. "So you're done here?"

"I'm done."

"It was always a long shot. My guys are combing the city. If the perps are still here, we'll find them."

Denison pushed through the front doors to the city office building, blinked in the bright hot day, and dug his phone out of his pants pocket. He felt not empty, but at a distance from himself, as if his consciousness was separated from his body by some sort of translucent barrier. "Nicole, the Crenshaw guys you wanted me to look for on the security cameras? I think they have Ron."

"What?"

"Yeah," Denison said. "The image was fuzzy, but I think they took him from the casino complex and toward the airport."

"Are you sure?"

"Pretty sure. I'm guessing it was sometime during the last hour. Wounded-Bear was sitting right beside me, so I couldn't look any closer."

"Thanks."

"What are you going to do?"

"I'm going over there to find him."

"That's crazy. You said these guys are killers. Let me tell Wounded-Bear. He can send a security team."

"No. We need to keep the authorities out of the loop, remember? Our priority is to find the casket. Their priority is to hush things up."

"My team will be here tomorrow. Wait until then, and my people can go get him."

"I appreciate the offer, but I can't wait that long."

"You won't be helping if you get hurt yourself."

"That's a chance I have to take."

Denison put his phone back in his pocket. There was no reasoning with her. She was going to do whatever she thought was right whether it made any sense or not. Where had the day gone? He could hear the distant murmur of voices from the boulevard. His stomach growled. He didn't feel any better now than he had when he left the hospital. He knew he should eat something, but the idea of chewing and swallowing seemed impossible. He needed to call Skip and Bell, tell them what Dr. O'Brian has said, but he just wasn't ready to face them. They would have questions about the future, and he didn't have any answers. He wished there was another simple task to occupy his mind.

He walked down the sidewalk to the street. The sun felt like it was baking his brain. Had he really spoken with Dr. O'Brian that morning? Had she really told him Stacey was going to die? He hoped Nicole would be all right. What made her make the choices she made? He turned right when he reached the street. Had he really admitted to himself that he knew Stacey was going to die? Maybe he should go back to the hotel. He stopped and looked off into the distance, not seeing anything. His mind was blank. No. He was going to the hospital. He had to see Stacey. He didn't want to. He knew that she would still be a broken, wasted caricature of herself, but he had to go. There was just something about seeing her—he had to see her before he could do anything else. Just seeing her would give him the strength to keep going.

NICOLE RUSHED out of the Arrowhead Hotel with her Glock in her handbag and turned right to take the most direct route to the private airfield. That's where the Crenshaw guys would most likely have taken Ron. She hurried around the perimeter of the Rising Rapids Waterpark to get to the boulevard. Children were squealing as they came down the slides and splashed into the pools. Nicole blended in with the crowd in front of the waterpark, crossed the boulevard to the airport side, and jogged through the chain-link gate and down the alley between the painted sheet-metal warehouses adjacent to the airfield tarmac. The Crenshaw guys would want to question Ron before they killed him, so he was probably at the warehouse or at the airplane hangar. She hoped he was still alive. She wasn't sure what she would do if she found him. She couldn't take on all five of them. But if there were only one or two...

RON SAT on a rickety folding chair in the Crenshaw Industries warehouse next to the green locker where he and Nicole had found Rickover. The leader of Philips's crew, the black guy that the others called Gary, stood in front of him, his hands in the pockets of his black nylon jacket, a scowl on his face. To his left and to his right were Blond Crew Cut and Black Goatee. Black Goatee had Ron's Smith & Wesson in his hand. Another white guy, with a potbelly and a fresh black eye, stood just behind Gary.

"You've been a pain in my balls," Gary said, "stirring up the pot and making the natives restless, but I think we've finally got a use for you."

Ron shook his head. He guessed his chances of leaving alive were fifty-fifty. "It's going to be a mistake."

"You're made to fit."

"Really?"

"Oh, yeah. See, you killed Rickover for the Cellini casket, you disappeared, no one knows what happened. We put you deep in the ground in the desert—which is what somebody on my shit list was supposed to do with Rickover." He glanced at the guy sporting the black eye. "And the case is never solved."

Ron looked up into Gary's poker face, searching for a tell. "You're joking, right? Just trying to have some fun at my expense. You know Rickover was trying to run a sting on your boss. That's why you're here. With him out of the way, the only person who can testify against your boss is Mosley. You know she's got the casket, right? That she's trying to use it to blackmail the high roller Rickover tried to sell it to?"

"Mosley who?"

Gary's right eye twitched. Ron saw his chance. "Come on, you've got to sound more convincing than that. Right now, it looks like you killed Rickover, stole the casket from him, and handed it over to Mosley, who's trying to generate some income for you. It doesn't matter what really happened. That's what it looks like. Your boss sent you here to straighten things out. Before he was just linked to a theft; now he's linked to a theft and a murder. What's he going to say when he finds out you've put him in deeper, instead of getting him out of the hole?"

"None of that keeps us from killing you just to tie up loose ends."

Ron kept spinning. "You don't get it, do you? The casket has to go back to the museum. It's too famous to sell. All it's good for now is connecting someone to Rickover's murder. You need to get control of Mosley, if she's your guy. She's a loose cannon, threatening this high roller. NewTrust's starting to pay attention. Anything happens to him or his wife, it'll be raining cops and SEAL-team-trained mercenaries around here. And then your boss can forget about whatever's in his locker at the freeport vault."

"Maybe. Maybe not. Who's this high roller?"

"James Denison. His wife's in the hospital here."

"Still doesn't explain why I should let you walk."

Ron added the final twist. It was all he had. "I can keep Denison quiet. My woman's fucking him. She's got him wrapped around her finger. You get Mosley off his back. I massage his reality a little bit. NewTrust stays out of the picture, and we all walk away clean."

"Get up."

Ron stood up. Gary nodded at Blond Crew Cut, who punched Ron hard in the stomach, knocking the wind out of him. Ron folded up. Black Goatee punched him in the kidney while he was bent over. He fell to his hands and knees. There was nothing more he could say. Blond Crew Cut kicked him in the side. He groaned and covered his head with his arms.

"That's enough," Gary said. He poked at Ron with the toe of his shoe. "You're on a short leash, asshole. You shut Denison up. You stay out of our way. You do anything I don't like; our next conversation won't end so well. Get out of here."

Ron climbed up the wall to get to his feet. He started toward the door and then turned. "Can I have my gun back?"

Gary started laughing as if he'd just heard the punch line to the funniest joke imaginable. The others just smiled and shook their heads.

NICOLE SLOWED down as she neared the Crenshaw Industries warehouse and began checking around the corners before she walked through the intersections of the streets and alleys. She wouldn't be able to help Ron if she got caught herself. As the warehouse came into sight, she saw the door open and ducked behind a dumpster. Ron stumbled out into the alley, rubbed his lower back and his shoulder, stretched his arms overhead, and started toward her, limping as he walked. She rushed to him.

"Ronny, what happened?"

"Blundered into Philips's crew." He bent over, put his hands on his knees, and shook his head. "How did you find me?"

"James saw you on the security cameras. You okay?"

"Yeah, I'm good. Did he see anything else?"

"He didn't say."

Ron stood back up. "Let's keep moving. They bragged about killing Aaron. I don't want to be here if they change their minds."

Nicole took him by the arm. "Are you really okay?"

"I'll be fine in a couple of hours. And it was worth it. I think I've got Mosley off our backs. Convinced them that she's the problem. And we've still got the car and Rickover's money. I spotted them first, so I dropped the car keys behind the trash can on the corner by our hotel before they grabbed me."

"Ronny, they could have killed you."

"But they didn't. I lost my .38, though."

"They handle it?"

He nodded.

"At least we don't have to worry about fingerprints."

They shuffled through the front gate of the private airfield and stopped on the sidewalk. "Do you need to rest?" Nicole asked.

"We need to keep moving until we're indoors."

"I might have a lead on the casket." She told him about following Clare to her condo.

"Your intuition is amazing, honey. The pieces of this puzzle seem like they're finally falling into place." At the first break in traffic, they crossed the boulevard from the airport to the waterpark. "And your work with Denison has been stellar. You should call him and tell him you're okay."

"After we pick up the car keys and get back to our room. I'll call him then."

9

CHANGING DIRECTIONS

L ater in the day, after Ron and Nicole showered and ate room service, they lay in bed with the curtains drawn, snuggled together. "You know, Denison didn't have to come down to the Nohamay Mountain Vault yesterday morning. He could have just let the security team deal with you," Ron said.

A satisfied smile crept across her face. "But he didn't."

"That was only because of the work you'd already put in." He shifted his weight so that he could look at her face. "Now he's almost one of the team. Taking our advice and providing information."

"You got a plan?"

"One thing at a time. We don't have the casket yet. I'm just saying that if the casket problem tidies up correctly, Denison is going to be in the palm of your hand. We just need to keep our eyes open for the right opportunity."

"Don't you think maybe he's off limits?"

"How's that?"

She sighed. "Not a player. Really didn't know the casket was stolen when he bought it."

"I know that's what he's saying, and he's saying it convincingly, by the way, and I know that you believe him, but the jury's still out as far as I'm concerned."

She shifted onto her back and looked up at the ceiling. "He's an emotional wreck."

Ron leaned up on one elbow. "I'm not saying we close the deal. I'm just saying that it's fair to make preparations until we know for sure. Particularly when it's not any extra work."

"If that's all you're saying."

"That's all, baby. You know how I feel about stealing from civilians. I got no problem taking the hundred thousand from Rickover, on the other hand."

"Yeah, I'm with you there. It was Denison's originally, but we didn't have anything to do with that." She looked for his eyes. "Say, maybe Mosley would take the ninety thousand for the casket."

"If we can't find it, I'm willing to try anything."

Nicole rolled toward the window. The lower part of the curtain glowed bright. "Sun's going down."

"Then I guess we better get moving."

They got up and put on comfortable, dark-colored clothes. Nicole checked over the Glocks and then opened a map on her smartphone and pointed out Clare's condo. "That's where we're going."

They went out of the front of their building and immediately turned right to go north, away from the casino. Two blocks later, they walked by the Tall Mesa Shopping Center, a small strip mall consisting of a drycleaner, a grocery store, and a hardware store that catered to the locals. Nicole looked at her map. They turned right on the next street. Down the block they could see a row of stuccoed condos.

"If we're lucky, Clare will be at work," Nicole said.

As they neared, they saw that the lights were on in Clare's condo. They went up to the door and knocked. No one came. Ron noticed a doorbell and pressed it twice. They could hear the bell easily through the door. No one came. Nicole banged on the door with her fist. They waited a few more minutes. Clare opened the door, dressed in her work clothes. "What?"

Nicole showed her Glock and pushed Clare back into the living room, Ron close behind her. Clare looked from one to the other. "Who are you? What do you want?"

Ron gave her a hard glare. "You're a player. You might not be in this game, but you're a player." He pointed to the sofa. "So sit down and be quiet, and we'll be in and out of here."

Clare sat down on the sofa with her hands in her lap. "You can't treat me like this. I'm protected."

"I'm sure you are, which is why we're so polite. If you've been minding your business, you've got nothing to be afraid of." Ron turned to Nicole. "I'll watch her."

Nicole walked back through the condo. In the living room/dining room, there were a sofa, two chairs, a flat-screen TV, and a square dining table with four chairs, but no Cellini casket. She went into the bedroom. There was a king-size bed, two bedside tables, and a wide dresser with a mirror. Clothes were tossed over a tan, overstuffed chair in the corner. She glanced in the bathroom: shower/bath combo, double sink vanity. She stepped into the walk-in closet: shoe boxes on the upper shelf, hanging clothes, two suitcases on the floor. They were empty. She came out of the closet and looked under the bed. Dust bunnies. She went into the bathroom and opened the double doors under the sink: toilet-bowl cleaner, a toilet-bowl brush, and a plunger. She came back out into the bedroom, looked behind the door, turned, and looked back at the tan chair. She dragged it out from the corner. Behind it was a red, wheeled suitcase. She rolled the suitcase out into the room and opened it. The casket lay nestled in packing foam. She closed the suitcase and rolled it into the living room. "Let's go."

Ron looked at Clare. "You know what's in that suitcase?"

She shook her head. "It's not even mine."

"Smart money would forget all about it."

Ron rolled the red suitcase out onto the sidewalk. He and Nicole hurried away, cutting down an alley to avoid the Tall Mesa Shopping Center, with its traffic and security cameras. They stayed in the dark as much as possible. A few cars drove by in the distance, and a coyote peered at them from behind a group of trash cans, but there were no people on the street. The only noise was the sound of their steps and the whir of the suitcase wheels. When they came to the parking deck where Ron had left the Camry, they each took an end of the suitcase and lugged it up the stairs. The beat-up Camry was still sitting where Ron had parked it. He turned off the alarm, unlocked the trunk, and checked to see that the gym bag of money was still in the wheel well, before they set the suitcase inside.

He smiled. "I don't want to jinx this, but I think I'm finally getting a good feeling about this project."

"We driving tonight?"

He shook his head. "I don't know how reliable this car is, and we don't have a spare tire. Wish I'd known that when I was at the auto parts store. Don't want to be stuck on the side of the road in the desert in the middle of the night. First thing in the morning will be soon enough."

After Ron reset the car alarm, they went down the stairwell on the far side of the parking deck, circled around the block, and cut through an alley to walk up to their hotel as if they'd come from the opposite direction. Ron looked into the hotel lobby before he opened the glass door. All clear.

GRACE MOSLEY WALKED out of the Great Circle Casino Hotel and stood in the circle driveway looking up at the stars. There were a few cars driving by and a few couples strolling on the sidewalk, but the evening had turned quiet outside. Her window of opportunity was closing. If Denison wouldn't give her the $200,000 for the casket, she was going to have to give it to Philips's men or run with it, neither of which were good options. Aaron had overplayed his hand. His ex was a single mom now. But at least his daughters had a mom. If she screwed up, Kelly would be an orphan. A special needs orphan. She'd go back to that overcrowded public facility. She'd never progress to independent living.

Mosley walked on the sidewalk around the circle drive down to the boulevard. The breeze was stronger here, and she could hear the distant noises of the waterpark. Extorting Denison. She never would have thought when she joined the FBI that she would become a dirty cop. It was so easy to be pure when you could pay all your bills, when no one was counting on you. She'd given up Aaron to save her daughter. That's where lying down with Philips had led.

She couldn't be weak now. Aaron's murder might give her the evidence she needed to get Philips off her back, but if she gave him the casket, he would be in a stronger position to blackmail her to force her cooperation in the future. If she ran with the casket, tried to sell it on the open market, she would put her job in jeopardy and risk jail, and without the protection of her job, Philips wouldn't think twice about killing her.

The casket had to go to the museum. She didn't have any wiggle room. If she wanted to help her daughter and win her own freedom, Denison had to come through with the cash, and she had to find concrete evidence that proved Philips ordered Aaron's killing, not just speculation and correlation.

A white panel van squealed up to the curb in front of her. Two men jumped out of the back, a black man with a goatee and a white man with a blond crew cut. "Get in the van," the white man said.

Mosley spun on her heels. She made two steps before they pounced on her and dragged her kicking and screaming into the van. The white man pushed her to the floor and sat on her while the black man pulled the doors shut. Up in the driver's seat, a white man with a black eye was looking over his shoulder. As soon as the back doors clicked shut, he sped off. The blond man got off of her. She sat up and pulled her clothes straight. "Do you know who I am?"

He nodded. "Remember me from the other night in your room?"

She studied his face in the gloom, and then she glanced toward the driver. "Yes."

"Gary just wants to talk to you. Relax. If we wanted to hurt you, you'd be unconscious, and we'd have your gun."

They pulled up next to the Crenshaw Industries warehouse. The only light in the alley came from the warehouse windows. The blond man led Mosley inside, where Gary was standing next to the nearest loaded pallet of boxes. "Special Agent Mosley," he said, "glad you could find the time."

"Do you really think you can grab me off the street? Mr. Philips is going to hear about this."

"Is that a rhetorical question?" He took a step toward her. "You've crossed the line. We know you already have the casket."

Mosley didn't say anything.

Gary nodded. "That's right. We know. You're going to give us the casket to take to Mr. Philips, and you're going to leave that Denison guy alone. You're stirring up a bunch of bullshit with NewTrust that's going to blow back on Mr. Philips. You're going to stop right now."

"I'm stirring up shit? Who botched up getting rid of Rickover?"

"All the more reason there's not going to be any more fuck-ups."

"I don't have the casket."

"Don't lie to me. You're not good at it, and you have too much at stake."

Mosley glanced back toward the warehouse door. The blond man stood there with his arms crossed and a blank expression on his face. They weren't going to let her leave until she agreed to do what they said. She turned back to Gary. "Okay. I'll bring the casket to you first thing in the morning."

Gary shook his head. "You'll go get it now. In the morning, you're getting on the first flight out to Charles Bay."

"Okay."

He stepped in close, grabbed her chin, and pulled her face up to his. "Look at me," he said. "This is my serious face. Do I look like the kind of man you want to fuck with?"

His breath felt hot. His eyes were like small black stones. She felt a chill run up her spine. "No."

He let go of her chin. "Don't make the mistake that Rickover made. Do what you say you're going to do. Bring me the casket."

The blond man drove Mosley back. They rode in silence, the blond man driving like a grandpa on his summer vacation and Mosley looking out the passenger window at the knots of people on the street as if she might recognize someone. When he pulled to a stop at the top of the circle drive to the hotel, she climbed out. "Tell Gary I'm going to be a little while."

"You've got his number?"

"Yeah."

"Don't be too long. You might be a special friend of the boss, but even that will only carry you so far."

She went into the lobby. A large group of people in formalwear were milling about as if they were between the wedding and the reception. She squeezed through them and down the hallway to the elevators, which led to a side door. The street was dark. She walked north toward Clare's condo, angling right and left through side streets so that she could be sure that she wasn't being followed. How did Philips's men find out she had the casket? NewTrust wouldn't have told them. That left Denison and the Carters, which meant that the Carters must have found a way to put Philips's crew on her to further their own plan.

Because they didn't want Philips to get the casket. They wanted it returned. Or so they claimed. But now they were just as screwed as she was. She couldn't help her daughter if she were dead, and it was clear that Gary thought he could kill her and get away with it. She would have to come up with a new plan to get free of Philips and get the tuition money.

She unlocked the door to Clare's condo and went inside. Clare was sitting on the sofa in the living room, looking off into space, a large whiskey in her hands. "I thought you had work tonight."

Clare stood up. "A man and a woman came here, threatened me with a gun, searched the house, and took a red suitcase I've never seen before."

"Red suitcase?" Mosley ran back into the bedroom. The over-stuffed chair was still pulled out from the corner. The suitcase was gone. She went back into the living room. "How long ago?"

"An hour, maybe."

"Oh, God." She sat in the chair facing Clare and held her head in her hands. "A man and a woman, dark hair, fortyish, fiftyish."

She nodded. "What's going on here, Grace? What have you got me involved in?"

Mosley looked up at her. "There's something in the suitcase that I was holding for Philips. I left it here because I thought it would be safe."

"Why didn't you tell me?"

"I thought it would be safer—that you would be safer if you didn't know about it."

"Because it's always better not to know if people might come to hurt you." Clare drank down her whiskey and set the empty glass on the end table.

"It's not like that. I trust you, Clare."

"If the suitcase belonged to Philips, why didn't you give it to his people?"

"That's what I was here to do, right now. Philips's guys are expecting the suitcase right now."

Clare looked down at Mosley and shook her head. "You're caught up in something, Grace. You're not making sense. You could have given the suitcase to the guys as soon as you got it. You brought it here to hide it. That's why you didn't tell me." She shook her finger at her. "You're going to tell me the truth right now. You're going to tell me the whole truth or you're going to get out of here."

Mosley looked at Clare's shoes. She spoke slowly and carefully. "My daughter is developmentally disabled. I can't afford the care she needs on my salary. That's why I work for Philips, to pay the tuition. But Philips is asking me to do things I can't do; it's just too much, so I was looking for a way out."

"Christ, Grace, you thought you could keep Philips's money or whatever, and he wouldn't find out?"

"The guys were tipped off about the suitcase. I'm supposed to bring it now. If it was still here, I could talk my way out of this."

"But the man and the woman took it."

"Exactly. So I'm screwed. The best I can hope for is that Philips thinks I'm more valuable alive than dead."

Clare knelt down in front of her and took her hands. "Do the guys know where you are?"

She shook her head.

"You lied to me. You put me in danger."

"I know. It wasn't what I intended. I thought you'd be safe from Philips if you didn't know, but you're right; I was a fool."

"You don't really love me, do you?"

"I never lied to you. I always enjoy our time together, but I only come here when Philips sends me."

Clare's lower lip quivered. "And that was never going to change."

"It's okay," Mosley said. "I'll leave." She started to stand up.

Clare put a hand on Mosley's shoulder. "I don't know why I should care about what happens to you after what you've done, but I don't want you to get hurt. You can stay here tonight, but then you have to go."

"You're a better friend than I deserve," Mosley said.

10

RUNNING THE GAUNTLET

Mosley woke up in Clare's bed. She could see the dim, early morning light through a gap in the bedroom curtains. Clare was turned away from her, breathing softly, her bare arm clutching the flower-patterned comforter up to her throat. Mosley slipped out of the bed. She quietly picked up her clothes from the overstuffed chair and padded out into the bathroom.

As she dressed, she mulled over her options. Her original plan was a nonstarter. Philips's men would kill her as soon as they found out she couldn't deliver the casket. They'd do a better job of dumping her than they had Rickover, and she'd never be found. And even if she were found in the bottom of some narrow gulch, there would be no evidence connecting Philips to her murder. To have any chance of saving her life and protecting her daughter, she needed to get away from Nohamay City and get back inside the safety of the FBI's bubble, which meant that she had to do her job—return the casket to the museum.

She tucked in her shirt and zipped her pants. But even if she managed to find the Carters, take back the casket, and escape the city, Philips would still be after her. And how far would he go to get even with her? Would he use the evidence he had against her to burn her with the FBI? Could he do that without implicating himself? Maybe she could still develop hard evidence connecting Philips to Rickover's murder and use it to strike a deal with Philips.

She splashed cold water on her face, patted her face dry with a hand towel, and looked at herself in the mirror. So many ifs, buts, and maybes. Avoid Philips's men, take back the casket, get the evidence against Philips. No matter what happened, she still needed Denison's money. Denison was just another rich asshole who thought rules didn't apply to him. He deserved to pay the $200,000 for trafficking stolen art. He wouldn't even miss the money. She brushed her hair and put on some lipstick. Out in the living room, she put her pistol in a holster at the small of her back and slipped on her suit coat. She thought for a moment of leaving Clare a note—a heart with a few lines of thanks inside—but what was the point? She'd burned her bridges here when she'd involved Clare in her trouble.

She shut the front door as softly as possible, and then pushed on it to make sure it was locked. The streets were quiet. The day felt new and somehow hopeful, even if this was the point of no return. First order of business was to get Denison's money, which meant going to the hospital, since that was the most likely place to pick him up without running into any of Philips's men.

Mosley arrived at the hospital with a to-go cup from the Caffeination coffee shop. She entered through a side door and went up the stairwell to the second floor where she peered through the wire hatching in the glass window of the fire door. The hall was empty, and she couldn't see anyone at the nurses' station by the elevators. She slipped down the hall to Mrs. Wert-Denison's room and peeked inside. She was asleep, emaciated and yellow-tinged. Mosley couldn't help feeling sorry for her. She should have been dead weeks ago. Mosley went back the way she had come and stood in the stairwell sipping her lukewarm coffee and watching the hallway through the fire door window, waiting for Denison.

A security officer, a full-figured Native American woman wearing silver and turquoise earrings with a navy-blue pants suit, sauntered down the hall and stopped outside Wert-Denison's door, where she leaned against the wall. She had a pistol and pepper spray holstered on her hips.

Mosley grimaced. The last thing she needed right now was interference from the NewTrust Corporation. She'd hoped to stay under their radar. Maybe the officer wouldn't be there when Denison arrived. Maybe when she showed her badge the officer would defer to her authority. But no matter what happened, she had more to fear from Philips's men than NewTrust. She had to get the money, get the casket, and get gone. She studied the security officer. There was no way of knowing her level of experience. If Mosley attacked, would she flinch and duck or would she overreact and pull her weapon? Mosley knew she was probably faster and more skilled, but the officer was larger and obviously stronger. She certainly couldn't take her in a straight-up fight. But maybe she wouldn't have to. She sipped her coffee and waited.

A while later, Denison, disheveled and spent, slouched down the hall and into the room. The security officer went into the women's restroom. Mosley opened the fire door and padded down the hall. The door to the room was open. Denison sat on a chair next to the bed facing his wife, his back to the door. He was talking on the phone. "She's unconscious. She's not going to wake up. It's just a matter of time now." He paused. "I love you, too." He put his phone back into his pants pocket.

"Denison," Mosley said.

He looked over his shoulder. "What do you want?"

"I'm here for the two hundred thousand."

"I'm not paying you anything."

"It will cost you more than that to clear up the scandal. Philanthropist caught up with art theft ring. That's a story with legs."

"Please leave us alone."

"So you'd rather make your family suffer?"

The security officer stepped into the room, her hand on the butt of her holstered gun. "Who are you?"

Mosley showed her ID. "Special Agent Mosley, FBI."

"What are you doing here?"

Denison pointed at Mosley. "My wife is dying. Make her leave."

Mosley replied to the officer, "I'm here investigating the theft of an art object."

"Be that as it may, no one's allowed in here. You're going to have to leave."

"I need to ask Mr. Denison some questions."

"And I have my orders." The officer gripped Mosley's arm and pulled her toward the door.

"This is a mistake."

"Take it up with Mr. Chen."

Mosley glanced at Denison. There were no options left. She had to have that money. She knocked the officer's arm free and grabbed for the pepper spray holstered on her belt. They fell back against the wall by the door, struggling over the pepper spray. Denison crouched by his wife's head, holding her hand in his. The officer pushed off from the wall and shoved Mosley across the small room. Mosley banged against the other wall and scrambled to her feet, the pepper spray in her hand. The officer reached for her gun, but Mosley pepper-sprayed her in the face, moving toward her as she backed into the hallway while trying to protect her face with her hands. The officer fell down on her hands and knees, gasping for breath, tears streaming down her face. Mosley took the officer's pistol, rushed back into the room, grabbed Denison by the arm, and pulled him into the hallway.

Denison looked at her as if she were crazy. "Where are you taking me?"

"You just couldn't cooperate, could you?" She dragged him down the hallway past the nurses' station and down the main stairwell to the first floor. Another security officer, a white-haired senior with a big belly, came jogging down the hall toward them. Mosley jerked Denison's arm. "Quit dragging your feet."

She pushed him into the hospital administration offices. Two women—one a Native American twenty-something, the other a middle-aged white woman—looked up from their computers. Mosley held up the security officer's pistol for them to see. The young woman squealed.

"Everybody out," Mosley yelled.

The two women jumped up from their desks and ran. Dr. O'Brian came out of her office, her white coat fluttering behind her and her reading glasses in her hand. "What's going on here?"

"Please," Denison said, "I need help. She's crazy."

Mosley pointed the pistol at O'Brian. "Shut up and get out of here."

O'Brian stammered, her eyes glassy with fear. She held her hands up and slowly backed out of the office.

Mosley pointed to an office chair that had rolled back to the far wall. "Sit down."

Denison sat. Mosley put the pistol into her jacket pocket and pushed the nearest desk up against the door. "What a fucking mess. Sorry if I scared you. I don't want to hurt you."

"You've got a strange way of showing it."

"Yeah, well, events got ahead of me. Like you, I've got family I'm responsible for, family I have to protect. They have to come first. Get me the two hundred thousand, and you'll be back with your wife before you know it." She took out her phone and called Gary. "Hey. You know who I am?"

"Where's the casket?" Gary said.

"There's been a change of plan. I'm in the hospital admin offices. Denison is with me. City security has me boxed in."

"You don't listen at all, do you?"

"The Carters stole the casket from my hiding place. You're going to get it from them and bring it to me. It's going back to the museum. And you're going to let me get on a plane, or I'm going to call in the FBI, and Philips's operation blows up."

"You call in the FBI, and you go to jail."

"But I'll still be alive. And you bastards won't have any hold on me. Find the Carters. Bring me the casket. It's your only way out."

. . .

RON AND NICOLE were in the beat-up Camry. They had just come through the drive-through of a Caffeination coffee shop. They each had a large black coffee and an egg-and-bacon croissant. Ron turned left on Mountain View Road and drove past the gas station where he had bought the car, but he didn't stop. His gas tank was full. At the next traffic light, he would make a right turn onto Trade Memorial Highway, the only road to Camp Carson, which was the nearest city outside the Nohamay Nation. Rickover's $90,000 and the Cellini casket were hidden in the trunk under their luggage and an assortment of junk that had been left in the Camry when he bought it.

In the rearview mirror, Ron saw a white panel van coming up fast. He turned on his right turn signal as he approached the traffic light. The panel van roared by them, braked hard, and slid sideways in front of them. Ron hit the brakes and turned to the right to avoid hitting the van. The Camry bumped over the curb onto the sandy right-of-way. Ron glanced in the rearview mirror. A blue van was behind them. Philips's men rushed out and came up to both sides of the Camry, guns drawn. Ron lowered his window. "What's up, guys?"

Blond Crew Cut squinted in the bright morning light. "Get out. Her, too."

They got out of the car. The men herded them back to the blue van. Gary was sitting in the front passenger's seat, blowing on a cup of coffee. "You two leaving town?"

"We're all done here."

"What a coincidence. Mosley has Denison. They're barricaded in the admin offices at the hospital."

"That's a tough break. Word gets out of the city, it'll make you guys look guilty."

"This is your fault."

"I just told you to warn her off. I don't know what you did."

"You have to give up the Cellini casket."

"We don't have it."

Gary nodded toward the Camry.

Ron smiled. "If we did have it, you don't think we'd be stupid enough to carry it with us, do you?"

"We could beat the information out of you, but the clock's ticking. So we're just going to hand you over to Mosley."

"What good will that do?"

Gary shrugged. "Buy some time to think of something better. Maybe we could spend some quality time with your wife while you babysit Mosley. Maybe she knows where the casket is."

Gary called Mosley on his cell phone.

"Yeah?" Mosley said.

"We got Carter for you."

"I don't want Carter. I want the casket."

"He claims he doesn't have it."

"Not my problem."

"Really? How do we know you even told the truth? Could be that your girlfriend is holding it for you."

"She's not my girlfriend. She works for the boss. She's got nothing to do with this."

"Just keep repeating that; you might start believing it. She's connected to you, so she's going to pay. I don't have to tell you how this works. You're wearing your big girl pants. Anything that's not completely clear eventually gets cleaned up. The boss won't take the chance, not even for family."

"You're making a mistake."

"If you're not lying, you show good faith."

"Okay. Send Carter to me. He better be able to help."

Gary ended the call. "All fixed up. You're coming to the hospital."

"Look, we don't know anything about the casket," Ron said. "Mosley is just blowing smoke."

Gary chuckled. "The bullshit never ends with you, does it? Get back in your car. You try anything stupid, you'll suffer a long time."

Ron and Nicole got back into the Camry, bounced down the curb onto the street, and made a U-turn. The white van was ahead of them and the blue van behind. "Listen," Ron said, "we're going to be there in a couple of minutes. I'm going to go into the hospital office and work on Mosley. We'll see what kind of rhythm that gets us."

"What's the play?"

"You stick with the car. Do the car thing. I'll drive Mosley and Denison to you."

"Denison?"

"Mosley's not going to give him up. He's her only leverage."

"But Denison is a civilian."

"Yes, he is. Doesn't mean he can't owe us."

"This is awful risky."

"We can't trust Mosley. We're not giving her the casket."

"What if she goes off the deep end?"

"Do what you got to do. The desert is full of arroyos."

"What about Philips's crew?"

"This is the only way to get away from them. We can't outgun them."

"You mean it's the only way for me to get away from them. What about you?"

"Don't worry about me. I'll take care of me. See you on the other side."

She reached over and gripped his hand. "I love you."

"I love you, too," he said.

MOSLEY HELD the curtain open a few inches with the barrel of the pistol and peeked out the window in the back of the hospital administration offices. City security officers, orange vests on over their blue blazers, were spaced about twenty feet apart all along the sidewalk, forming a perimeter. She assumed it was the same in the front. She wondered how they were spinning it to hospital patients and visitors. Special emergency drill? She walked back to the front of the offices. Denison was still sitting in the office chair against the far wall.

"How do you expect to get out of here?" he asked.

She peeked out the window into the lobby. It was empty. She could see a lot of activity on the front lawn, but she couldn't make out the details. "They can't just light up this place and murder me here. It's too public. As long as I'm here, and I've got you, I'm safe. They're going to do what I want. You're going to get me my money. What's two hundred thousand to you?"

"I'm not going to help you."

"Stop kidding yourself. You're going to do whatever you need to do to get back to your wife." She pointed to the front door. "Philips's guys are going to bring Carter to me. He's going to give me the casket. You're going to get me my money. We're going to ride to the airport and get on a plane together. No one will try to harm me as long as I have you with me. As soon as we land, you're on your own."

"I'm not leaving my wife here. I'm not leaving her to die alone."

The telephone on the nearest desk rang. Mosley picked it up. "Yeah?"

The voice spoke with a slightly Asian accent. "This is Mr. Chen. If you don't release Mr. Denison immediately, we will contact your superiors."

"You want to open that can of worms? Rickover's murder, stolen art, and contraband in the Nohamay Mountain Vault? This place will be swarming with federal agents. You'll be able to count your guests on one hand. The Nohamay Nation will void your contract. No. If you want this to end, you're going to help me get my two hundred thousand dollars and the object the Carters stole from me. Until then, quit bothering me." Mosley hung up.

Ron PARKED in the parallel parking in front of the hospital, which was cordoned off with yellow tape. Security personnel wearing SWAT gear stood in clumps, walkie-talkies in their hands. A black mobile command truck sat on the grass near the front steps. Mr. Chen stood outside the truck talking with Wounded-Bear, a Native American woman wearing a doctor's white coat, and a small, thin white woman wearing a gray-blue skirt suit. Ron looked at Nicole. "Looks like the usual shit storm in progress. There should be lots of opportunity for us." He separated the car keys from the car alarm remote and handed the remote to Nicole.

"Be careful," she said.

"You know what to do."

Nicole slid down in her seat. Ron moved away from the car as quickly as he could without acting suspiciously. Philips's men hurried from their vans and started after him. The nearest security officer, a hard-muscled Native American with a crew cut, looked him up and down.

"Mr. Chen is expecting me," Ron said.

He kept ahead of Philips's men, forcing them to focus on him while Nicole rolled into the backseat of the Camry. When they all reached the mobile command truck, Mr. Chen turned toward Ron and pointed his finger. "You always seem to be wherever there is trouble. I told you to leave town."

"That's what I was trying to do."

Chen looked at Philips's men. "I don't know who you are. Why are you here?"

Gary put on an earnest expression, his hands in the pockets of his black nylon jacket. "We want the same thing you want, Mr. Chen—to get Denison out of there and to get our hands on Mosley."

Wounded-Bear gave Gary and his men an appraising look. "I know what you guys are. You're going to surrender your weapons. Then you're going to get back behind the police tape."

Gary continued. "Do you have the Cellini casket? 'Cause that's what Mosley wants. She sent us to get it back from Carter, but he claims he doesn't have it. So we brought him."

"Mr. Rose is Mr. Carter?" Chen asked.

"Exactly. He's the one."

Wounded-Bear snorted. "That's your plan?"

Gary nodded. "Trade Carter for Denison and let Mosley deal with him. You got a better idea?"

Wounded-Bear turned to Chen. Chen looked off at the front of the hospital. "These incidents of the last few days, if not properly contained, will seriously impact our business interests. Agent Mosley cannot leave unless we let her. We want to avoid the controversy of involving her superiors if we possibly can. Mr. Denison must not be harmed." He turned back to the others. "We don't care what happens to Mr. Carter. So we will give him to Agent Mosley. Maybe that will satisfy one of her demands. She also wants two hundred thousand dollars." He turned to the woman wearing the blue-gray suit. "Joyce, call Mr. Stands-Alone. Tell him to expense the money out of the casino and send it here immediately. We need to get Agent Mosley out of here as quickly as possible."

Wounded Bear shook his head. "Giving in to her demands is a bad idea. We should see if a sniper can get into position."

"We are not giving in," Chen said. "I won't risk Mr. Denison's life. Once we have him, we'll deal with her." He turned to Ron. "Mr. Carter, do you need an escort or will you go inside on your own?"

"I'll go."

Wounded-Bear put his hand on Ron's shoulder. "Up against the truck."

"What?"

"We're not going to have any surprises."

Ron put his hands on the side of the mobile command truck and spread his legs. Wounded-Bear patted him down. "He's clean."

Chen called Mosley. "We're sending in Mr. Carter."

"Okay," she said.

Ron walked up the steps and into the lobby of the hospital. Security officers peered out from behind barricades in the hallways. He knocked on the door to the administrative offices. The curtain gapped at the window. Ron could see the barrel of a pistol. He held up his sports coat and turned in a circle. The door opened. Mosley stuck a pistol into his chest and pulled him into the room. "Sit down." She directed him to a chair placed next to Denison. Mosley locked the door and pushed the desk back in front of it.

"You're a tricky man, Carter," she said.

"I don't know about that."

"Where's the casket?"

"I don't have the faintest idea."

"Bullshit." Mosley sat on the edge of the desk, the pistol resting on her thigh.

"You think I don't want out of here?" Ron asked. "Why should I care if you get the credit for returning it? All Denison and I want is for the casket to be returned so we can get on with our lives. I don't know what you've gotten yourself into, but right now I'm just like you, stuck between Philips's crew and the city security forces."

"Really?"

"I was on my way out of town when they caught up with me."

"So you do have the casket."

"No, but I still have my life, and I was hoping to keep it. How were you planning to get out of here?"

"Plane."

"Really? Aren't you concerned you'll just be arrested or murdered after you land?"

"I'm the FBI, Carter. Why would I be arrested?"

"Kidnapping?"

"Denison can't say a thing. He'll be inconvenienced, but at the end of the day that's all it will be." She went to the window and peeked out. The lobby was clear.

"Let Denison go," Ron continued. "Chen is putting together two hundred thousand as we speak. He's willing to pay that just to get rid of you and shush this whole thing up."

Denison clasped his hands together. "Come on, Agent Mosley. You said you had family that's important to you. My wife doesn't have much time. I need to be with her right now."

"I wish I could help you, Denison, but I can't. They won't shoot at me if they think they might hit you. So I can't let you go until I'm safe."

She turned to Ron. "You were on your way out of town? They didn't get you at the airport?"

"No, I bought a car. Not much to look at, but I think it will take me across the desert as far as Camp Carson, anyway."

"All loaded up?"

"I was almost at the city limits when Philips's guys put a road block on me."

Mosley studied Ron's face. He was quite the liar. The Carters took the casket. They wouldn't leave it here. If Philips's men or NewTrust had it, she'd know about it. So if it wasn't in checked baggage at the airport, it had to be in their car. "Then I'll take your car. Safer than standing around at the airport." She turned to Denison. "I'm not an asshole. I want to help you. We take the car, and you'll get back quicker."

"It's not for sale," Ron said. "It's my only way out of here."

"I'm not buying it. I'm taking your car and everything in it. That's my price if you won't give me the casket."

"I don't have the casket."

"There you go." Mosley picked up the desk phone and speed-dialed the last caller. "Carter has a car on the street out there?"

"Yes," Chen said.

"Put five gallons of water and the two hundred thousand in it. I'm taking Denison with me."

"You cannot take Mr. Denison. I will go with you, and he will stay here."

"And I'll be dead before I reach the city limits. No, Mr. Chen, Denison stays with me until I'm off tribal land. I won't harm him if I don't have to. My career is on the line. But if you follow me or shadow me with an airplane or interfere in any way, all bets are off. Call me when the water and money are in the car." She hung up.

"I won't go with you," Denison said. "I have to stay here."

"I'm sorry, Denison," Mosley said, "but you're going. It's just a matter of how comfortable you're going to be. And the more you drag your feet, the longer it takes. Cooperation is the fastest path back to your wife."

"You're not taking my car," Ron said. "I can't afford to buy another one."

Mosley shook her head slowly. "I'm the one with the gun, Carter. I'll do whatever I like. You, I'm not the least bit sorry about. If Aaron hadn't known you, he might still be alive today."

"What are you talking about? He's the one got me and Nicole involved in this mess."

"Yeah, but fooling with criminals is what got him believing in his crazy scheme. Give me the car keys."

. . .

Twenty minutes later, Chen called. Mosley came out of the hospital with Ron and Denison in front of her, her pistol in Denison's back. She scanned the hospital grounds. Ron's Camry sat by itself at the curb. The security personnel stood in a knot near the mobile command truck, their pistols holstered and their assault rifles pointed down, but Mosley wasn't taking any chances. She needed to move fast. If anyone was going to try to stop her, now was their best opportunity. She hurried Denison along, keeping in close behind him.

Chen called out to her. "I have done everything you asked. Please reconsider taking Mr. Denison."

"Sorry, Mr. Chen. We both know that's not possible." She turned to Ron. "Go over there with the rest of them."

Mosley and Denison continued to the Camry. She pulled open the front seat passenger's door and motioned for Denison to get in. "You've got the money," Denison said. "You don't need me."

"I wish that were true."

"I can guarantee your safety. Just leave me here."

"Get in."

Denison sat down in the car. Mosley handcuffed him to the door handle. "Relax. You'll be free in a few hours."

Mosley scurried around the Camry and climbed in. She called out to the command truck. "Where's the water and the money?"

Wounded-Bear replied, "In the back seat."

She reached into the back seat and unzipped a black canvas bag. It was full of banded bundles of hundred dollar bills. A five-gallon jug of water sat on the floor mat. She smiled to herself. And the casket was hidden in here somewhere. It had to be. All the breaks were finally lining up her way.

Ron stood with the others at the mobile command truck and watched Mosley drive off. It was all up to Nicole now. Chen turned to the Native American woman wearing the doctor's white coat. "Dr. O'Brian, please reopen the hospital as quickly as possible."

"Do you want them followed?" Wounded Bear asked.

"Why? The road only goes to Camp Carson. Call the tribal police. Have them call us when they see Mosley and Denison cross out of tribal land. Then get this mess cleared up." He turned to Joyce. "Let's go back to the office."

O'Brian hurried up the steps to the hospital. Chen and Joyce headed off to their car in the parking lot behind the building. Wounded-Bear frowned at Ron. "Did you forget about our conversation yesterday?"

"As quick as I can find transportation, I'm gone."

Wounded-Bear turned to Gary and his men. "I guess you gentlemen came here on a private jet. You've got two hours to get back on it. Your kind isn't welcome here."

Gary grinned, his hands in his jacket pockets. "I'm sorry you feel that way."

Wounded-Bear climbed into the mobile command truck. Ron started down the sidewalk. Gary called after him. "Where are you going?"

"We're all done here, aren't we?"

"Where's your wife?"

"I haven't got the slightest idea. She's got to be here somewhere. Can I go now?"

"No, you're coming with us until the boss tells us how he wants things handled." He turned to his men. "Find the wife. Bring her to the hangar."

MOSLEY DROVE the Camry past the city limits sign on Trade Memorial Highway. The small, rundown houses at the edge of town disappeared in her rearview mirror, and the desert stretched out in front of her. Two hours to the northeast, the city of Camp Carson lay just outside of the tribal lands. As soon as she got there, she was going to drop Denison wherever he wanted, and then she was going to take the car apart, find the casket, and book the earliest flight back to Charles Bay. Once she was clear of the Nohamay Nation, Gary's threats were meaningless. She could return the casket to Peter Damascus, take the victory lap, write up the evidence connecting Philips's men with Rickover's murder, and begin the process of pinning Philips into a corner just tightly enough so that he would decide to leave her alone instead of trying to blackmail her or kill her. And the $200,000 would buy the time she needed to find a new income stream to pay Kelly's tuition. She glanced at Denison, who was leaning against the door he was handcuffed to and looking out the window at the dry shrubs and cactus flying by.

"You okay?"

"I'm never going to forget that you dragged me away from my wife."

"I'm sorry about that. I really am. But I didn't make your wife sick, and I didn't involve you in a crime. You got yourself involved, and this is the price you have to pay. Make the best of it. At least you aren't going to jail."

The highway was hot, dusty, and marred by potholes. There were no rest stops or convenience stores on the two-hour stretch. Tribal members seldom went down to the casino city, and most of the tourists flew in. Mosley tried to steer onto the best part of the road as she sped along, but the contents of the trunk banged about whenever they bounced through a rut or worn-down patch on the road. Still, she didn't slow down. She wanted to be in Camp Carson as soon as possible. She had no idea how long it would take Philips's crew to get started after her, but she knew they weren't going back to Philips empty-handed if they could avoid it. He wasn't the kind of boss who forgave mistakes. About forty-five minutes out of Nohamay City, the Camry's engine sputtered and died. The gas gauge indicated full. Mosley steered onto the shoulder. She put the Camry in park and turned the key. The starter clicked, but nothing happened. She pumped the gas and tried again. Nothing. "I can't believe this."

Denison smiled grimly. "Can't get where you need to go? Welcome to my world."

She popped the hood and got out of the Camry. There were no cars in sight—not even a dust cloud that might indicate a possible distant car. She lifted the hood. Everything was fine as far as she could tell. Maybe the starter was defective. Maybe if she banged on it a few times, it would reset. She went back to the trunk to look for a hammer or a heavy wrench. She turned the key in the lock and lifted the lid. Nicole lay on her side pointing her Glock at Mosley's abdomen. "Hands up, one step back."

Mosley stepped back with her hands in the air. "How did you do it?"

Nicole climbed out of the trunk, careful to keep her gun pointed at Mosley. "Remote car starter with a starter disconnect. I turned the car off and locked out the starter."

"What now?"

"I don't care about you. You can have the water and the money. I'm taking Denison and the car."

"Out here, without the car, Philips's guys or NewTrust will just come and collect me."

"You can put on the handcuffs and ride back with us. Take your chances with NewTrust. Maybe they'll put you on a plane."

"I can't do that."

"Really? You think they'll kill you?"

"They've got no reason to protect me from Philips's men."

"Then I guess you're walking. Maybe someone will pick you up, take you to Camp Carson for a hundred dollars."

Denison yelled, "What's going on back there?"

Nicole glanced over her shoulder. "We're going back to town."

Mosley crouched, quick-drew her pistol, and fired. The bullet grazed Nicole's neck and went through the open trunk lid. Nicole fired as she turned back. The bullet pierced Mosley's right shoulder. Her gun fell from her hand. "Jesus." She stooped to snatch up her gun with her left hand, but Nicole hopped forward and kicked her in the face, knocking her onto her back.

"Stop it," Nicole yelled. She stood over Mosley with her gun pointed at Mosley's chest. "Are you really that desperate? You got nothing to live for?"

Mosley lay on her back, momentarily dazed, her right shoulder pounding. She put pressure on the wound with her left hand. "Okay," she said. "Okay."

Nicole picked up Mosley's gun and put it in her belt. She touched her neck wound and looked at the blood on her hand. "Where's the other gun?"

Mosley started to lie, but knew she'd be frisked anyway. "Right-hand pocket."

Nicole took the security officer's pistol out of Mosley's jacket pocket. "Stay still. I'll see if I can find the first aid box."

She went around to the passenger's side, opened Denison's door, and uncuffed him. "Where did you come from?"

"I was hiding in the trunk."

"You're bleeding."

"It's nothing."

"Did the others know?"

"Only Ron."

He pulled his phone out of his pants pocket. He didn't have any reception. "Let's get out of here."

"Got to patch up Mosley first."

"She'll make it back."

"Maybe, but I don't want to have to explain a dead FBI agent. Chen would try to get on the right side of that problem by feeding me to the Feds. Help me find the first aid kit."

They dug around in the trunk until they found the first aid kit and a ragged gray blanket. They spread the blanket on the gravel shoulder in the shade of the car. "Mosley, can you get up?" Nicole asked.

"Yeah."

"Come over here to the blanket. If you try anything, we'll get in the car and leave you here."

"I'll cooperate," Mosley said. She rolled onto her side and crawled up off the ground.

Nicole opened the first aid kid to see what she had to work with. It was out of date, but it was the full kit for a hunting or backpacking trip. Mosley lay down on the blanket. "Okay," Nicole said. "I'm going to pull your jacket off and have a look. Turn on to your side."

Nicole peeled off Mosley's jacket, and pulled her bloody shirt down her shoulder. The wound was just to the outside of her bra strap. It wasn't bleeding too badly. Nicole swabbed the blood from the wound on the front and back and examined it. The bullet had gone all the way through. "Not too bad." She turned to Denison. "Could you hand me a couple of gauze pads?"

She put the pads over the entry and exit wounds and taped them into place. "That should hold you until you can get to a hospital." She helped her sit up. "Are you coming back with us?"

"Let's go," Denison said. "We're wasting time."

"I can't go back there," Mosley said. "Leave me with the money and the water."

Nicole shook her head. "You forfeited the money when you shot me. Happy to leave the water."

"You'd leave me here shot, without the money?"

"You tried to kill me. Sorry, your choices suck."

"Leave the water. Please."

Denison pulled the five-gallon jug from the backseat and placed it beside Mosley. "I'm going to make it out of here," she said.

"I hope so," Nicole said. "I have James as my witness that I patched you up and offered to take you with us."

"You're a bitch."

"Come on," Denison said.

Nicole used the remote to reconnect the starter. She made a wide U-turn and started back toward Nohamay City.

Mosley sat in the gravel beside the road watching them drive away. Her shoulder was pounding. She'd lost the casket and the money. She was on foot in the middle of nowhere. It no longer mattered if she could put together definitive proof that Philips had Rickover killed; she couldn't afford to quit him now—not if she wanted to keep Kelly at Clear Skies. She tugged her bloody shirt up over the bandages on her shoulder. She needed water. She uncapped the water jug, lay down next to it, and tipped the opening to her mouth. Water sloshed down the side of her face, but she drank and drank until she felt too full. She sat up and capped the jug. The water that had run down her face had immediately disappeared into the gravel. The sun seemed powerfully hot. She pulled her jacket over her head to protect her face. There was a leathery shrub nearby, creating a small pocket of shade. She dragged the water jug to it, and lay down with her face in the shade. She needed to rest for just a few minutes—just long enough to get her strength back—and then she would have another drink and try to walk to the next shady spot. She had to keep trying. She couldn't give up. Kelly was depending on her.

NICOLE SPED DOWN THE HIGHWAY, weaving through the potholes, pushing the old car past its limit, the rpms in the red zone. As long as she didn't blow it up or wreck it, it was worth the gamble to get back as soon as possible. Denison had his phone out, trying to call the Nohamay Alternative Medicine Hospital. This was his third try, and he still didn't have any reception. They had the windows down. The hot wind roared through the car, roiling bits of grass, miscellaneous wrappers, and grit into the air. Nicole glanced at him for a second. "Let me get a little closer."

He set his phone in his lap. "It's been over two hours since I've seen her."

"I know," she said.

"I've got to know how she is."

"I know."

He looked at his phone. One bar. Maybe it was enough. He raised his window and dialed again. "Hello? Wert-Denison's room, please." He waited to be connected. "Dr. O'Brian? Yeah, this is James Denison. I'm on my way back now. Maybe," he glanced at Nicole, "thirty minutes. What? I'm sorry; the reception is bad. Say again." He held the phone tight against his ear. His voice dropped. "No. It can't be. I'm almost there." He set his phone in his lap and leaned against the window. "She's gone."

Nicole slowed down and pulled over on the gravel. She put the car in park. Denison was quietly crying, tears running down his face. She put her hand on his shoulder. "I can't imagine how bad you feel."

"I never should have brought her here."

"You were trying to do the best that you could with a hopeless situation."

He took out his handkerchief and dried his eyes. "I need to call the kids."

"Wait until we get to town. It's not much longer. You'll have good reception there. Your call won't be interrupted."

He put his hands on the dash, dropped his head between his arms, and started crying again. "I've got to think of what to tell them."

"Just tell them the truth. You did everything you could."

"She was the best wife, the best companion, the best lover."

Nicole reached over and rubbed his back. The words just fell into her mind. Very softly, she said, "You're making me jealous. Nobody ever loved me that much."

He turned his head to look at her. Her eyes were bloodshot and a tear trickled down her cheek. She sniffed, smiled with embarrassment, and put her hands in her lap. He sat back, wiped his face, and blew his nose. "How do you do that? How do you make such a blunt observation seem so supportive?"

She wiped her cheek with the palm of her hand. "Ready to go?"

He nodded. She pulled back onto the road, driving a little more carefully than before. There was no rush now. Neither of them spoke until they passed the city limits sign. "Do you have the casket?"

"I know where it is."

"So you are stealing it."

She shook her head. "It has to go back to the museum. We can't be connected with a missing art object. It's like I've been telling you all along—we can't live with that kind of exposure."

"Well, you rescued me, so on that basis I'm willing to trust you."

"Take you back to the hospital?"

He nodded.

"I am so sorry about your wife. The way you've cared for her; I know she was a very special person."

They pulled up to the curb in front of the hospital. The mobile command truck, the yellow tape, the security officers were all gone. All that was left of the morning excitement was a bruised lawn. "Well," Denison said, "I guess this is good-bye."

"I have to get out and look for Ron."

As they got out of the car, three men dressed in dark suits, with the look of ex-military about them, hurried over. The one in the middle took off his sunglasses when they reached Nicole and Denison. "Mr. Denison? I'm Joel Fredricks with Manifold Security." He took his ID out of his suit coat and handed it to Denison.

"I wish you had been here a little earlier."

"Yes sir. I'm sorry for your loss. There's two men upstairs. And a Dr. O'Brian wants to speak with you."

Denison handed the ID back to Fredricks.

"Have you seen Ron Carter here?" Nicole asked.

"Ron Carter?" Fredricks paused. "I'm sorry, I'm just trying to get up to speed here. I believe he left with a group of guys right after Mr. Denison drove away with Agent Mosley. Where is she, by the way?"

"Last we saw of her," Denison said, "she was sitting by the highway. She didn't want to come back with us." He turned to Nicole. "What are you going to do?"

"I've got to see if I can help Ron."

"You three go with her. I'm going to see my wife."

He started up the sidewalk. "Wait a minute, James." Nicole climbed into the backseat of the Camry and came out with a black canvas bag. "You forgot this."

"What's that?" Denison said.

She handed him the black bag. "It's the two hundred thousand."

He looked at her and then at the bag and then at her again. "You certainly are full of surprises. But it's not mine. NewTrust provided it. I'll see they get it back."

·   ·   ·

Ron sat on a straight-backed wooden chair in the Crenshaw Industries airplane hangar. He knew most of the names of Philips's men now, which wasn't a good sign. Gary, Jacob, and Charles were loading weapons and tactical gear onto the plane. "How much longer do I have to sit here?" he asked.

Gary looked up after he finished tacking the lid on a wooden crate. "When we get a call back from the boss, we'll either leave you here or bring you with us."

Mitch and the big black guy with the glasses came into the hangar. "Couldn't find her anywhere," Mitch said. "And the security cops were dogging us every step of the way."

Gary turned back to Ron. "Where's your wife, Carter? You're not worried about her, so you must know where she is."

Ron looked at the men in the room. Were they going to let him go, kill him, or take him with them and make a decision later? It was always easier to transport an ambulatory person if you could get their cooperation. You could take them right to the place where you wanted to dump them. No heavy lifting, no leaking fluids, no smell. And a dead man is a lot harder to explain at a roadblock. For now there was nothing he could do. He was outnumbered, and if he ran, he'd just be forcing them to kill him to be on the safe side.

Gary's phone rang. "Yeah?" He listened for a moment. "Right, boss." He paused. "That's the situation. We've been ordered out. You'll have to send somebody else."

The hangar side door opened. Fredricks and his two associates, Kevlar vests over their shirts and ties, spread out into the hangar with their pistols drawn, Nicole right behind them. Philips's men drew their pistols. "Hold on, boss," Gary said.

Nicole spoke. "Ron's coming with us."

Gary told Philips what was happening; then he handed the phone to Ron. "He wants to talk to you."

Ron took the phone. "Yeah?"

"Have we met before?"

"I don't think so."

"But you know who I am?"

"I do now, Mr. Philips."

"You stepped all over my business there. That's not something I forget. Staying out of my way is your best health-care decision."

Ron handed the phone back to Gary. "It's me, boss," Gary said. He listened for a moment and then put his phone back in his pocket. "You can go."

Ron and Nicole backed out of the hangar, covered by Fredricks and his associates. "These are Denison's guys?"

"Yeah."

"How is he?"

"He's all broken up. His wife passed while he was gone."

"And you're the hero."

They all climbed into a white Suburban. Ron and Nicole sat in the back with Fredricks. She explained what happened.

"How's the car?"

"Needs some gas."

Ron turned to Fredricks. "Thanks for the save there."

"Just doing what Mr. Denison asked me to do."

"Thanks, anyway."

Fredricks dropped Ron and Nicole off next to their car in front of the hospital. They got in the Camry, Ron in the driver's seat. "There's only an hour of daylight left. Do we still have the casket and Rickover's ninety thousand?"

"They're still in the trunk."

"What about the two hundred thousand?"

"I thought it was Denison's."

"That's okay, honey. Chen wasn't going to let us keep it." He put the car in drive. "Mosley was alive when you left her?"

"Alive and moving around."

"Let's get some gas and get out of here before anybody changes their mind."

They drove down Trade Memorial Highway. The sun was falling in the west, casting a red glow behind the low, brush-covered mountains. Long shadows fell across the chaparral. The heat reflecting off the road created a watery mirage that stayed in the far distance directly in front of them. "It was just around here somewhere that we stopped," Nicole said.

Ron slowed down. They were both looking at the right side of the road. "There's the water jug," Nicole said. She pointed at the five-gallon jug lying on its side near a small leathery bush. "Up ahead. That dark-colored lump."

Ron pulled over. Mosley lay on the side of the road, face down, her good arm flailed out like she had collapsed while crawling. Nicole jumped out of the car and ran to her. She put two fingers to her neck, feeling for a pulse. "She's still alive."

Nicole rolled Mosley over and lifted her head into her lap while Ron got a water bottle from the car. He handed it to her. She wet Mosley's lips, and then sprinkled water on her face. Mosley opened her eyes. "You came back." Nicole held the bottle to her lips and let her drink. She took a few swallows, and then she pushed the bottle away. "You're wasting your time. I won't go back to the city."

Ron crouched down beside her and gripped her hand. "We aren't going back."

She looked at him hard. "Where's Denison?"

"You've been out here on the road for a couple of hours. Denison is back in the city. Did you know Philips's guys were going to kill Rickover?"

She tried to sit up. Nicole helped her. "Not until it was too late. He was a friend of mine, you know? That's why I wanted the money, so I could get out from under Philips's thumb. That's why I can't go back to the city. I'm dead there."

Ron turned to Nicole. "Take a look at her shoulder."

Nicole gingerly lifted the outer bandage. The bleeding has stopped. "It looks okay."

"Can you walk?" Ron asked Mosley.

"I think so."

He turned to Nicole. "Let's put her in the car."

They helped her to her feet and walked her to the Camry. She lay down in the backseat. "You okay?" Nicole asked.

"Yeah," Mosley said.

"We'll take you as far as the hospital in Camp Carson," Ron said.

They continued down the highway, the light disappearing over the mountains, the valley falling into the deep shadow that comes before true night. Ron turned on the headlights. The world was empty except for them driving through the dark and the sky slowly filling with stars. Mosley sat up in the backseat. "Why are you helping me? I shot her."

"Yes, you did. And if you'd killed her, I'd be hunting you right now. But we're not psychos," Ron said. "Besides, you being dead doesn't help us. If you're dead, we've got even more Feds on this case. Since you're alive, you're going to make sure we aren't tied to the theft of the casket. A deal's a deal."

"Easy for you to say. What am I going to do about Philips? I don't have any money."

"NewTrust has the two hundred thousand, so at least they're not after you. As for Philips, you're the FBI. You'll think of something."

It was well after dark by the time they saw the lights of Camp Carson. A tribal police cruiser sat on the shoulder of the road at the border of the Nohamay Nation, but it didn't stop them from crossing into the city. The streets were deserted. They rolled through the commercial zone, passing the twenty-four-hour big box stores with their nearly empty parking lots, and stopping at the empty intersections to wait for the traffic lights to change.

Nicole looked up from the map on her phone. "Next right should be the hospital."

They drove in the emergency department entrance. Ron pulled right up to the double doors. "Can you make it?"

"I can make it that far," Mosley said. She opened the car door and put one foot out onto the pavement before she turned back to Ron. "Have you got the casket?"

"It's going back to the museum," Ron said. "It's going to mysteriously turn up in the next few days."

"Then I'll keep my word." She stumbled out of the car, righted herself, and shuffled toward the emergency department doors.

11
PROMISES KEPT

Ron pulled up in front of the Peter Damascus Sculpture Museum on a Harley Davidson motorcycle and parked in the do-not-park zone with the hazard lights flashing. He was wearing a black-visored helmet, heavy leather gloves, and a black leather jacket with the logo "Quicksilver Messengers" on the back. He unstrapped a rectangular wooden box from the back of his bike, hurried up the steps to the Spanish-style mansion and walked into the glass-walled addition where the entrance and ticket counter were located. He didn't bother to take off his helmet or his gloves. He looked up at the security camera as he approached the ticket counter. Two twenty-something women were chatting behind the counter. He set the box on the counter without speaking.

"Do you need a signature?" one of them asked.

He shook his head.

"Thanks," she said.

He jogged back down the steps, climbed onto his motorcycle, and roared off down the hill.

Two days later, Ron and Nicole were standing at the kitchen

counter of a beach house on the coast well north of San Francisco. The waves were rolling up the beach, washing against the rocks, and leaving seaweed on the gravelly sand. Dirty breakfast dishes sat on the picnic table on the wooden deck. They were on their way back outside with refilled coffee cups, but they had stopped to watch a news story on the TV in the kitchen. The TV showed a rotating view of the Cellini casket, while the voice-over told how an anonymous messenger had returned it to the Peter Damascus Sculpture Museum. The museum's curator and the board of directors were ecstatic at its return. The FBI was still investigating the theft, but there were no new leads.

Ron sipped his coffee. "So far, so good." He turned off the TV. "Now everything is back to normal."

"Have you gone over the plans Zeb dropped us?" Nicole asked.

"Yeah. There's a bank up here that's really just a marijuana money-laundering operation. We've got the plans, the alarm codes, the armored car pick-up dates—everything you could need if you wanted to take some of that money."

"But they're independents, right? It's not some cartel enterprise?"

Ron smiled. "Actually, it belongs to our old friend, Mr. Philips."

"Are you insane? We just escaped from him. You can't leave well enough alone, can you?"

"He's using an old-timey, third-rate vault. And the armored car isn't even supposed to carry cash. He deserves to be robbed."

"Go look in the mirror and tell me if you don't see an idiot."

"When I've got a scab, I've got to pick it." He took her hands in his. "Think about how much fun this is going to be. All that easy money and the blind rage Philips is going to feel when he's been robbed, and he doesn't know who did it. It's the kind of good feeling that makes me want to give some money to charity."

She pulled her hands out of his. "Don't try to sweet-talk me. I'm not an adrenaline junky. You want me on this, the plan better be fool-proof—no almosts or maybes. Completely, absolutely foolproof. Every contingency covered."

"Of course, baby. Of course. You know me. Belt and suspenders."

"We'll see."

12

BANKER'S HOURS

A month later, Ron and Nicole, each wearing dark coveralls over their street clothes and carrying a large black duffel bag, came out of the service door into the alley next to the First Marine Bank. It was 2:00 a.m. They were right on schedule. The dark in the alley was as thick as dirty oil. Ron used a small flashlight to light their way. Nicole had broken the street lamp in the alley before they went into the bank. An old Dodge minivan was parked with the passenger's side against the far wall of the alley. Ron lifted the back, heaved in his duffel, and then took Nicole's and heaved it in. She hopped into the back. Ron walked around and climbed into the driver's seat while Nicole climbed over the seats to the front passenger's seat.

Ron pulled up to the end of the alley. The street was deserted. He took a right, got in the left turn lane on Beaverdale Street, and stopped at the red light. A police cruiser pulled up beside them. The green arrow for the left turn came on. They turned onto Tulip Avenue. Nicole looked over her shoulder. The police cruiser went straight through the intersection. They took the next right and pulled into a parking deck behind the Spring Valley Mall. On the third level, they parked the minivan next to a blue Prius, moved the duffels into the Prius and drove away. Just as they were leaving the parking deck, they heard police cruiser sirens, first one, then another, and then another.

"That's all three police cars," Nicole said.

Ron drove through an industrial area, past the razor-wire-topped chain-link fences of a scrap-metal recycler and an auto salvage yard, and into a nearby residential neighborhood of doublewide mobile homes and small, one-story houses. Two forty-five a.m.

"Easy as pie," Ron said.

"We're not gone yet."

Soon they were flying down the coastal highway back to their rented beach house. It was a moonless night. There were no other headlights in sight. They pulled up into their gravel driveway and parked beside a black Ford Explorer that was facing out. Ron transferred the duffels to the Explorer. Then they peeled off their coveralls and gloves and put them in a garbage bag. "Touch anything in the Prius?" Ron asked.

"Never took my gloves off."

"Keep your eye out for a picnic area with a trash can."

They got into the Explorer and headed down the coast toward San Francisco. The surf crashed against the rocky beach. The clouds drifted, revealing some patches of stars. Nicole's phone rang. It was three-thirty in the morning. She glanced at Ron.

"Who is it?"

"Don't know. Should I answer it?"

"Better. If it's suspicious, we want to toss the phone."

She put the phone up to her ear. "Yeah?"

"Nicole?" Denison asked.

"James. How did you get my number?"

"I've got my ways."

Nicole sat back in her seat and put her feet on the dash. "Is it morning where you're at?"

"Just finished breakfast."

"How have you been?"

"I'm doing okay, I guess. They say it gets easier, whoever they are."

"Yeah, that's what they say."

"I saw on the news that you returned the casket."

"That's what we said we'd do." She turned to look out her window into the night, but all she saw was her reflection in the glass. "I'm kind of busy right now. Is there something you need?"

"No, I just wanted to talk."

"It's good to hear your voice, James. Call me another time when I have time to chat." The line was quiet. "James," Nicole asked, "are you okay?"

"Yeah, I'm okay. I was just wondering—this might sound a little weird—but I was just wondering if you'd like to meet me in Cricket Bay?"

"Cricket Bay?"

"It's in Florida. I own a little place there."

Nicole put her hand on Ron's arm, shook her head, and smiled. "That depends. When did you have in mind?"

"Sometime in the next week or two, I was hoping."

She added a purr into her voice. "And what did you have in mind?"

"Hey, come on, you know me. It's not like that. I was just hoping we could continue our conversation—get to know each other better."

"James, you need to find someone to put you off this plan."

"Why's that?"

"You know who I am, and you know what I do."

"I'll take my chances."

"You'll take your chances?"

"I will."

"Can I reach you at this number?"

"Yeah."

"I'll call you back."

Ron glanced over at her. "So, spill."

"He wants me to meet him at his Florida house."

Ron chuckled. "I knew you were that good. No one can do the girl next door better than you. You are a deal-closer."

"What do you think?"

"Are you kidding me? You got to meet him."

"He knows who we are."

"He thinks he does."

"You're not suggesting we play him?"

"No. He's a civilian. But he might make a useful friend."

"I don't know. His kids could get in the way. They'll mark me for a gold digger without even meeting me."

"Worst case scenario? You spend some vacation time practicing your craft. There's no downside here."

"I just don't understand what your angle is."

"Honey, I don't always have to have an angle. Give him a call. Unless you don't want to."

"No. He's fun to be with."

"Then call him back. We'll have this money stashed by tomorrow. I can work up another job while you're off playing girlfriend."

"You're not going to be jealous, are you?"

"Honey, I'm happy for you. There's never anyone between us. Have fun."

"Okay. I'll tell him yes."

Ron looked down the highway into the dark beyond the headlights. If everything stayed on course, maybe Denison could be her retirement plan. It would be hard to go on without her. She was without doubt the best he'd ever worked with—the only one he'd ever truly loved—but an opportunity like this was once in a lifetime. He couldn't let her pass it by.

"Excellent. That's what you should do. Tell him yes."

A Note from the Author

Thanks for reading *The Freeport Robbery*. If you enjoyed it, please post a review on a review site of your choice. A few words will do. Honest reviews are the number one way I attract new readers.
Thanks so much.

I'd love to hear from you. You can reach me at my website: https://michaelpking.org.

The Travelers

The Double Cross: A Travelers Prequel
The Traveling Man: Book One
The Computer Heist: Book Two
The Blackmail Photos: Book Three
The Freeport Robbery: Book Four
The Kidnap Victim: Book Five
The Murder Run: Book Six